The Secret Life of Saeed
the pessoptimist

The Secret Life of Saeed
the pessoptimist

by Emile Habiby
translated by S.K. Jayyusi and T. LeGassick

Interlink Books
An imprint of Interlink Publishing Group, Inc.
Northampton

This edition first published in 2003 by

INTERLINK BOOKS
An imprint of Interlink Publishing Group, Inc.
46 Crosby Street, Northampton, Massachusetts 01060
www.interlinkbooks.com

Library of Congress Cataloging-in-Publication Data
Habibi, Emile.
[Waqa'i' al-gharibah fi ikhtifa' Sa'id Abi al-Nahs al-Mutasha'il. English]
This secret life of saeed the Pessoptimist / Emile Habiby ; trans. by Salma Khadra Jayyusi and Trevor LeGassick.—1st American ed.
    p. cm. — (Emerging voices)
ISBN 978-1-56656-415-1
  I. Jewish-Arab relations—Fiction. II. Jayyusi, Salma Khadra. II. LeGassick, Trevor. III. Title. IV. Series.

PJ7828.B53 W313 2001
892.7'36—dc21   2001039601

Printed and bound in the United States of America

Cover painting "Woman," 1988, by Masudul Hassan,
courtesy of The Royal Society of Fine Arts, Jordan National Gallery of Fine Art,
Amman, Jordan.

This English translation is published with the cooperation of PROTA (the Project of Translation from Arabic); director: Salma K. Jayyusi, Cambridge, Massachusetts, USA.

Contents

Book Two: Baqiyya—the Girl Who Stayed

Book Three: The Second Yuaad

INTRODUCTION

The novel is a new genre in Arab literature, mainly the outcome of this century, and its rootlessness can be traced to particular circumstances in Arab literary history. After the great artistic and intellectual achievements of the long period of time between the sixth and fifteenth centuries A.D., Arabic literature suffered a long period of stagnation. This was precisely the same period in which European literature was steadily progressing and developing its fictional genres. When the Arab literary renaissance began in the nineteenth century, poets found in the old poetic tradition a great wealth to build upon. From an artistic point of view, the initial return to the old poetry was inevitable if the hackneyed and benighted verse, which had been inherited from the age of stagnation, was to find renewed strength in language and style, a strength that could only be drawn from the best examples in the same language. The interest in the novel, on the other hand, became a serious involvement only in this century. The fact that Western fictional genres were highly developed by then, and that they were relevant in style, theme, and spirit to modern times, was an attraction that seemed to furnish a shortcut to modern literary methods, and the Arab writers, aspiring to attain a modern spirit in literature, tried to make the transition directly, rather than build on the fictional tradition of a medieval literature rich enough for its time. This was encouraged by the fact that the various fictional genres in Arabic had not been rooted in a continuous tradition in formal literature as securely as poetry had been. For all their popularity and wide dissemination, the *Tales of the Arabian Nights*, transmitted in a language that was infiltrated by the vernacular, were never elevated to the rank of fine art, which stipulated purity of language and grandeur of address. Other genres such as the allegorical story (represented by *Kalila Wa Dimna,* a collection of great interest assembled in the eighth century by Ibn al-Muqaffa'), and the picaresque (represented by the famous *Maqamat* of al-Hamadhani (died circa A.D. 1008), and al-Hariri (died circa A.D. 1123) which were fictional-comic representations revolving around the personality of the trickster) were not revived by modern writers as a possible foundation for modern Arabic fiction. In fact, it took creative prose writers in this century many decades before they felt confident enough in their art to fall back on classical prose literature, one of the richest in the world, and take inspiration from its universal and timeless aspects.

With only a few exceptions, modern Arab writers were consistent in their choice of tone and mode. Whether they wrote in the romantic or realistic tradition, in the tragic or heroic mode, they favored a serious tone and a direct approach. The comic apprehension of experience, burlesque and parody, double meaning, the picaresque, the ironic and sarcastic, were not easily adopted, and the richness of both classical Arabic and Western literatures in these modes was rarely utilized. The greatest exceptions to this are Abd al-Qadir al-Mazini (d. 1949), Tawfiq al-Hakim, and Emile Habiby in this novel. There seems to have been some impediment that prevented most writers from finding a way to apprehend the comic spirit in literature as they sought to depict human experience at a time of great political and social upheavals. One explanation for this may be the fact that as a new literary genre, modern Arabic fiction suffered for several decades from the uncertainty and weaknesses inherent in a newly adopted genre. The art of the comic is difficult to accomplish, and the adoption of a comic mode for fiction was delayed until the genres of fiction were able to establish themselves on firmer ground. It might also be that the comic apprehension of experience belongs to a more sophisticated period where writers have a clearer insight into the human condition, a more philosophical concept of life, and a deeper knowledge of the absurd and the paradoxical. In classical Arabic, for example, the pre-Islamic period of the fifth and sixth centuries had very few experiments indeed that revealed a comic apprehension of the human condition. However, when the Umayyad's had established an Islamic empire (661–750) and Arab tribes were settled in the newly founded towns, poets demonstrated the great scope of the comic, and the famous satires that rang throughout the epoch often contained a hilarious invective. However, it remains true, as one peruses the vast panorama of Arabic literature, that the tragic spirit is more spontaneous with the Arabs, while the heroic, so muted in modern Western literature, is even more constantly alive in their hearts.

The *Pessoptimist* is an account spanning over twenty years and two wars (1948 and 1967) in the life of the Palestinian Arab population, which remained in the State of Israel after the mass exodus following each war. The author, therefore, uses the fictional mode to describe some aspects of contemporary history. His aim, it is clear, is to give some details of the hardships, the struggle, and the underprivileged status of the Arabs in Israel, not through the drier medium of a plain historical narrative, but through the more sympathetic medium of fiction. He weaves a mesh of personal and fictional events around particular historical events and general conditions.

The use of a fictional mode for this purpose should not be seen as a necessarily less serious or, in its essence, a less reliable method of dealing with historical material. For although there is, in principle, a great scope for invention, improvisation, exaggeration, and over-characterization in literature, it all remains a matter of the author's choice, purpose, and manner of writing. The writer of fiction, moreover, has the prerogative of being able to focus on certain aspects of a human experience without being seen as willfully "suppressing" other details, since the prerequisites of artistic perfection rule out the inclusion of unnecessary material, the digression to irrelevant action or detailing, or the involvement on an equal level with all aspects of an experience. What one is dealing with in literature is not only or necessarily the recounting of events in their normal sequence, but the description of their *effect* on the characters of a fictional mode. In art, one can only focus on what happens to the limited number of protagonists in the particular literary work. Art, like memory, is never exhaustive; it is selective. As experience in actual life gets lodged in the mind, the memory "selects" and retains only some of its details. In the same way, the writer of fiction selects and brings into focus what he or she finds particularly outstanding in an experience.

But it is not only literature and art that are selective. Historiography itself is selective. In his essay on "Historical Texts as Literary Artifact," Hayden White attempts to show the great discrepancies among historical accounts of single events between one historian and another. He sees the writing of history as being similar to the relating of a story, which, by a process of "emplotment," as he terms it, is achieved in a great variety of ways. In this process, the historical account is determined by the language the writer uses to describe the event, and the figurative mode in which the account is cast: irony, metonymy, or synechdoche, et cetera.

As a writer of a historical novel, Habiby has the advantage of writing from the inside, experiencing firsthand not only the events of the period, but also the conditions under which the Palestinian Arabs have been living. A founding member of the Israeli Communist Party and a leading Arab Journalist, Habiby (born 1919) was elected three times to the Israeli Knesset, or Parliament, on the Communist list, and has been editor in chief of the leading Arab periodical inside Israel, the bi-weekly, *Al-Ittihad (Unity)*, on whose pages he has published a large number of editorials revolving around social and political issues. As a writer of fiction, however, Habiby became known on a pan-Arab scale with his collection of short stories on life in Israel after the 1967 Arab-Israeli War, *Stories of the Six Days* (1969). However, it is his novel *The Secret Life of Saeed, the Ill-Fated Pessoptimist*, (Haifa, 1974) that has won him the greatest acclaim. It ran into three printings in the first three years, and was reviewed in laudatory terms in numerous periodicals in the Arab World and in Israel. This unanimous welcome did not stem merely from the fact that it was an eyewitness account of the life of the Arabs in Israel, nor because it was the most prominent fictional work to speak about the crucial problem of Palestine and of the tortuous experience of its people; but also because, on an artistic level, it was highly original, fresh, and, being cast in the straight ironic mode of comic fiction, it was a challenge to the existing modes of fiction in the Arab World. It pointed to a new malleability, and it signalled the arrival of a new facet of maturity in the art of fiction writing in modern Arabic. The vision of Emile Habiby, as Trevor LeGassick rightly points out in his review article, "The Luckless Palestinian" (published in *The Middle East Journal*, vol. 34, no. 2, spring 1980) "is that of a mature and informed mind and the result of many years experience." In this novel, Habiby follows no set conventions, and, so far, his work has been inimitable. This contrasts with Palestinian Resistance poetry, which has already established its attitudes, its set range of themes, and has achieved a unified tone of either heroic resistant or, as we see in the most recent poetry of such poets as Mahmud Darwish, the major poet of the resistance, and others, a mixture of the heroic and the tragic. The ironic mode must be sought elsewhere in contemporary Arabic poetry: in, for example, the work of the Syrian, Muhammad al-Maghut, a poet who approaches the whole panorama of the contemporary Arab experience, including the Palestinian, with a fine, ironic sensibility.

The main character in the novel, Saeed the luckless pessoptimist, is a comic hero, a fool, in fact, who recounts the secrets of his life in the state of Israel in the form of a letter to an unnamed friend. This he does after he is safely ensconced somewhere in outer space in the company of an extraterresitrial being who had come to Saeed's rescue as he sat on top of a perilous stake, unable to move in any direction. Now, in the safety of his new home, Saeed can speak freely for the first time and the story he recounts is a heart-rending tale of defeat and rebellion, death and regeneration, terror and heroism, aggression and resistance, individual treason and communal loyalty; in short, of various aspects of a life lived constantly on the point of crisis. The paradoxical view of the dynamics of the situation explains the meaning of the word "pessoptimist," coined from the partial merger of "optimist" and "pessimist." Habiby aims to mix the comic with the tragic and heroic on the one hand, and, on the other, to uncover the various contradictions that crowd the distance between the extreme poles of Zionist colonialism and Palestinian resistance.

Enmeshed in the politics of the novel and its social complexities are the personal experiences of Saeed. He is an informer for the

Zionist State, but his stupidity, uncanny candour, and cowardice make of him more the victim than the villain. Despite his constant attempts to please the Establishment, he never succeeds in becoming an important member of the Zionist secret service and he is rarely rewarded for services performed. He remains a little man, an alienated and frightened soul living on the margins of life. His immediate boss, Jacob, is a Sephardic (Oriental) Jew with whom Saeed forms a lifelong friendship. Jacob himself is oppressed by his own boss, an arrogant Ashkenazi (European) Jew, referred to in the book as the "Big Man."

Our comic hero's only claim during the first two-thirds of the novel to a warm-blooded experience is his love for the first Yuaad, (after whom the first section of the book is named), and for Baqiyya (after whom the second section of the book is named.) The first Yuaad, whose name means: "to be returned," was his first love; he had known her during Mandatory Palestine, and continued to love and remember her with regret. She was evicted from Palestine and thrown outside the borders by the Israeli soldiers just after the formation of the Israeli State in 1948. She lives and dies in the diaspora and mothers the second Yuaad (after whom the third and last section of the book is named), and a heroic resistance fighter, also named Saeed, whom the Pessoptimist meets in an Israeli prison after 1967. Baqiyya, whose name means: "she who has remained," is one of the Arabs who remained in Israel in 1948. She becomes Saeed's wife and bears him his only child and son, Walaa. Baqiyya is in possession of a secret involving a treasure, which her father had buried in a cave in the sea, and Saeed spends his life looking for this cave. However, it is Walaa who secretly finds the treasure. Rebelling against the Israeli oppression of the Arabs, Walaa becomes a freedom fighter (a fida'i) even before 1967, and he uses the treasure to carry on his fight against the State. Habiby offers one of the most touching scenes in the novel when he describes Walaa, besieged in an abandoned house at the seashore by the Israeli soldiers, while his father, summarily called to the scene by the authorities, sits in silence on a rock, hunched and vulnerable, and his mother tries to talk him into surrender. The son's angry defiance reveals the agony of a tortured soul in rebellion. Baqiyya is moved deeply and joins her son. The last that is heard of them is that they were seen embracing each other and walking into the sea, which engulfs them.

However, it is his encounter in prison with his namesake, the heroic Saeed, that transforms the Pessoptimist. In the upheaval of the 1967 June War, the Pessoptimist, being the frightened fool that he was, makes an idiotic blunder, and is eventually put in prison by the Big Man who also hopes that he will be a seeing eye for the State among the prisoners. It is there that Saeed is brutally beaten by the Israeli gurads, and where he is laid next to the heroic Saeed who mistakes him for a fellow traveller, a freedom fighter like himself, and awards him the respect and affection which the Palestinians reserve for those who fight for freedom.

If Saeed is not a member of the resistance, his own son, Walaa, has been, and he has died a martyr for the cause, Saeed suddenly remembers with pride. Out of prison, Saeed finds that he can no longer collaborate with the State, and is put in prison several times. His meeting with the second Yuaad, a modern and courageous young woman who has entered Israel in accordance with the policy of the "open bridges" to look for her brother, only helps to confirm Saeed's stance.

However, his change of heart, although decisive for the severance of his relation with the Zionist State, cannot carry him much further. If he rejects his former role of informer, he is still crippled by his natural cowardice and limited intellect. The dilemma in which he finds himself is symbolized in the novel by the tall impaling stake on which he finds himself, and from which only a miracle can save him.

The language in the novel is, on the whole, simple and suited to the comic, as well as to the utterings of a simple-minded man. Habiby frequently incorporates words, phrases and proverbs from the Palestinian idiom. His style is succinct and emotionally restrained, yet suggestive. His tone is usually muted, and almost never lapses into the trap of rhetoric. Instead of the loud, direct tone of other literary writings that denounce aggression and glorify resistance, Habiby manages to accomplish the same with wit, irony, sarcasm, ridicule, over-simplified candor, understatement, double meaning, paradoxes, puns, and play on words. In this way he is able to present a refreshing formula for the reestablishment of faith in the possibility of freedom and liberty at the same time that he exposes the nature of the dilemma at whose core the tragedy of the Palestinians lies.

The Pessoptimist not only invites comprison with Voltaire's *Candide* (to which the author gives recognition in the novel), but also the Czech writer Jaroslav Hašek's *Good Soldier Schweik* (1923). Drawing a vivid comparison between Candide and Saeed, Trevor LeGassick shows how "the lucklessness, the innocence of their relationship with women, the foolish optimism, tactlessness and gullibility these characters share are remarkably similar." Schweik shares many of these qualities. Like Saeed, he is constantly preoccupied with the problem of defending his life against a petrified and cruel world. In this obsessive involvement to stay alive despite the gruelling death machine around them, both characters show no resistance or hatred, and neither express protest or objection. Instead, they wear the mask of the subservient Fool, all too ready to demonstrate an ardent obedience and a willingness *ad absurdum* to serve those who control their destinies. Saeed's exaggerated demonstrations of loyalty to the State, for example, are masked with innocence to appear true, but they convey the opposite meaning—the suggestion that a terrible punishment lies in wait for those who are not loyal. Never abusive, obscene, or violent, he relies on an attitude of assumed innocence, which pretends ignorance of the real issues, and by speaking with childlike naivete about these issues, he uncovers their horror and absurdity.

Because the comic hero deviates, by the nature of his role, from social norms, he leads an alienated existence: he is slapped, reviled, insulted, treated as an outcast, disinherited. Yet, he bears everything with the rigid patience of the wise Fool whose foolery is his passport to safety.

The figure of the wise Fool is not new in Arabic. One of the most beloved popular figures is Juha (the Arab counterpart of the Turkish, Nasr al-Din Khodja) who is sometimes depicted as a small man cunningly donning the mask of the Fool in order to protect his life. An anecdote about Juha and Abu Muslim al-Khurasani, the mighty commander who defeated the Umayyad dynasty in the middle of the eight century, is typical. It is said that Abu Muslim was curious to meet Juha and asked one Yaqtin ibn-Musa to summon him. Because of Abu Muslim's reputation for severity, Juha was naturally alarmed. On being presented by Yaqtin, Juha naively asked, "Yaqtin, which of you two is Abu Muslim?" Abu Muslim smiled, which he was not known to do.

Saeed, also being a wise Fool, saves his life by succumbing to the side that has the power, becoming an informer in the service of the State, which is the service of the enemy. The figure of the traitor-informer appears frequently in modern Arabic literature. For more than half a century he has been depicted as a vicious, cleverly self-seeking, and generally loathsome kind of anti-hero. He stands on the opposite side of the heroic character, who is proud, self-sacrificing, stoic, valiant, and undefeated even in death. The former walks toward the damnation of himself and the destruction of his people, and is never redeemed. The hero marches toward the noble goal of redemption by blood of both self and nation, and is regarded as immortal. The two are one-dimensional and rigidly fixed, the repetitive nature of their facile constructions making them artistically uninteresting.

Habiby flouts the rule. He makes it possible for both types to undergo a transformation. The dehumanized stereotype of the informer changes and assumes a more benign stance. It is true that the stock figure of the hero survives in young Saeed, whom the Pessoptimist reverently thinks of as "King." But the other heroic character, Walaa, the Pessoptimist's own son, who dies a martyr, is depicted in torment and agony, in rebellion against both the enemy and his own father and mother. This is a stance which causes him great suffering, at sharp variance with the unflinching and painless stance of the heroic hero elsewhere in modern Arabic literature.

Saeed is not the only comic figure in the novel. The personality of the "Big Man" is another archetype of the comic character. He represents the State (i.e., power), and he has an acute sense of the importance of his role. His rigidity and mechanical way of carrying out his job, his sense of his own grandeur, his blind and nervous drive to execute his "duty" at all times, his snobbishness and his over-reaction to the smallest aberration in the code of behavior he has fixed for his subordinates and for the Arabs, make a faithful picture of the buffoon who, unlike Saeed, arouses no sympathy in us.

Habiby has been able to see man in unheroic positions. If the core of the tragic world is a moral order corrupted by evil, then the world depicted in this novel is a closed one where two evils have met and where heroism has been born out of the havoc that has resulted from their meeting. The author implies that the Palestinian catastrophe is not an isolated phenomenon; war and aggression were not inflicted upon a progressive social order, but were the result of a double moral bankruptcy; the encounter of Israeli agression and reactionary Arab politics, with the latter represented first and foremost by the Arab upper classes in Palestine. In fact, Habiby seems to suggest that, in Trevor LeGassick's words, "a silent conspiracy based on the evident mutual material interests of the Arab and Jewish oligarchies of Palestine was a major factor in the creation of Israel. The sarcastic passing comments on their roles stand in strong contrast to the author's curiously lyrical praise for the Arab workers and peasants, who are depicted as the true builders of the roads and cities of modern Israel." In addition, Habiby "sharpens his keenest satirical barbs" for the Arab hierarchy of power outside Israel, and arrives at the logical conclusion that the Palestinians in the diaspora suffer the same tragedy as those inside.

But it is Israel's cruel policy as a settler state that is the main focus of his attack. Habiby explores the subject of cruelty from many angles. He fanatically avoids sensationalism, but in a matter of fact way, mixed with comic interpolations from Saeed, he tells the history of some thirty years of repression. The humorous style emphasizes by its very construction the paradoxes of the situation. Here, Habiby reflects a full understanding of the nature of institutional cruelty. Take, for example, the Gothic tale of horror that Saeed, in his understated way, describes as having been enacted on him in the Shatta prison. The "circle" of Israeli guards who victimize him are described as heartless and identical, acting mechanically like robots, "they were all tall and broad shouldered. Each one had sleepy eyes, arms at the ready with sleeves rolled up, thick, strong legs, and a mouth wearing a smile worse than a frown. They all seemed to have been formed in the same mould."

xviii

An image of a powerless world dominates a good part of the novel. A mechanized force is seen at work, blindly executing a policy of mass evictions, mass arrests, usurpation of property, and physical torture. Saeed, endowed with the cunning of the wise Fool and a keen instinct for self-preservation, realizes in the depth of his heart that under such institutional oppression a victim is, in Franz Fanon's words, "encircled . . . fragile and in permanent danger." His whole life is informed by this realization.

In addition to the three dimensions in the novel—the comic, the heroic and the sadistic—there is also a tragic dimension. Recent literary works revolving around the Palestinian experience usually end on a note of affirmation, but they can hardly escape a tragic realization of universal injustice. Habiby is no exception. His Saeed is a comic figure touched by tragedy. We can certainly detect in his light-hearted farces and occasional, comic cynicism, many references to the bitter tragedy that is being enacted daily on his people. The theme around which the novel revolves is a fit subject for tragedy: manslaughter, conflagrations, wars, rebellions, and all the chaos that accompanies such great upheavals in history. This is in the heart of modern literature. Comedy and tragedy in modern literature are no more regarded as antithetical genres as classical dramatic theory professed (Cicero: "In tragedy anything comic is a blemish and in comedy anything tragic is ugly.") Prominent writers like Thomas Mann rejected the old classification, asserting that modern art views life as tragicomedy, while Ionesco declared that he could never understand the difference between the comic and the tragic.

This is not to say, however, that *The Pessoptimist* is a tragicomedy in the full sense of the term. It is, rather, a political satire based on a comic apprehension of the human condition; it is touched by the tragic and heroic, and employs some motifs from the fantastic (the intervention of the man from outer space, for example.) Although he arouses our pathos, the Pessoptimist is not a tragicomic figure: he is not elevated enough to deserve the role. At the same time, the emphasis on the heroic mitigates the tragic aspect in a situation where death (of Walaa and his mother) is a choice, an act of willed rebellion that leads to elevation, not an inevitable end to a tragic fall.

But there are other similarities with tragedy in the novel. *The Pessoptimist* proves what has been said before: comedy has its own

catharsis. The novel is highly therapeutic. Through comic representations, it relieves much of the internalized tension caused by our
awareness of the presence of human cruelty and injustice. The comic
hero, moreover, can share the experience of his tragic counterpart:
a moment of discovery when one "sees things plain." This is the
Greek *anagnorisis*, and in Wylie Sypher's words, (appendix to *Comedy*,) "Comedy can have its *anagnorisis* too, when the foolish recognize their folly." In fact, Saeed experiences such a moment of recognition, which is then followed by a reversal of his stance. This is
another similarity to tragic reaction. Habiby has not chosen the
moment when Saeed's son and wife die for his *anagnorisis*. It would
not have been possible for the lifelong Fool to suddenly shed off the
rigidity, which Bergson describes as lying at the roots of the comic,
and which "compels its victims to keep strictly to one path, to follow
it straight along, to shut their ears and refuse to listen." Saeed,
despite his growing sadness after his family's tragedy, continues on
his former path, sustaining his character as the frightened little man
always ready to please his keepers. The full awakening of his consciousness takes place only after he has fallen victim to the scourge
of the Israeli prison guards; when, lying battered and groaning in
his prison cell, the other prisoner, the heroic Saeed, addresses him
as an equal. It is an unmerited homage and the Pessoptimist knows
it, but it awakens in him a new sense of dignity and restores his long
lost self-respect. This new situaation is at variance with all his past
humiliation, particularly that suffered at the hands of his own son
just before the son's death. The shame and self-rejection that he
experiences are counterbalanced by the new sense of his own humanity and by the sudden passion he feels toward this dignified and
stately figure, battered and blooded like himself, but bearing his lot
stoically (with the same courage that Saeed once saw in Yuaad's
eyes).

However, the fact that we "feel for him emotionally," as Trevor
LeGassick confirms, is not simply due to his reversal. Even before
this, we had felt sympathy for his tragedy, and pity for his victim-
ization at the hands of the instruments of the Establishment for
which he had slaved all his life. Stendahl says that we remain un-
touched by the plight of the comic figure, and our responses to both

Juha and Malvolio, for example, confirm this. We speak of Juha being robbed, cheated, reviled, terrorized, and even dying, without ceasing to smile. We cannot accept him as a man touched by sorrow, not in a way that arouses our empathy. The reasons why Saeed engages our emotions do not simply lie in the fact that he is not distanced enough to secure our indifference to the happenings in his world, but because we know that behind all this foolery he suffers from a real *dread* of a political order that has proven its ruthlessness. His naive admission, moreover, of his limitations and obsessive fears, his gentle manner, and his almost constant failure to cause real harm to others, arouses our sympathy for his predicament, even before he is reformed.

However, Saeed's reversal does not go much further than the shedding of his fool's mask and a refusal to collaborate with the State. What this situation achieves is a change in our attitude. We move from amused frustration and occasional pity to concern and compassion as we see him suffer the repeated punishments of the Big Man, who attempts to lure him back into his former role. In this particular aspect, Saeed ceases to be comic. (He does sustain a comic naivete in other instances, such as his blunders in the Village of Salakah.) As writers on the comic have emphasized, laughter precludes the presence of emotion. In this sense, Saeed's reversal and subsequent suffering change the mode of the novel to some extent.

Otherwise, Saeed's reversal does not, and cannot, furnish him with a solution to his misery. On the contrary, it lands him in an intractible situation. He has been entrenched in a position of security outside society: a spectator, indifferent to its misfortunes and caring only about his own personal safety. But now, a wish stirs in him to identify with the cause for which the younger man is struggling, and for which his own son has died. And it is when he yearns to be a part of the movement of Arab life, when he wants to *belong,* that he, ironically, loses his invincibility and becomes vulnerable.

At this point, being the eternal coward that he is, Saeed is unable to enter the struggle and has to face the contradictions of his situation. Incapable of resuming his old, despicable role, he finds himself trapped, and winds up on a symbolic stake, completely the victim of his own impotency. It is clear that only a miracle can save him now.

This comes in the person of the man from outer space, a symbol of metaphysical power. Sitting on that precarious stake, unable to join any of the people calling to him from below—his son, his wife, the two Yuaads, the heroic Saeed, Jacob, the Big Man—Saeed can only go upward, into Heaven, where no human problems can touch him. "Comedy tolerates the miraculous," says Wylie Sypher. Tragedy cannot accommodate a solution based on transcendental values, for it is of purely human substance. It is sharp edged and develops toward a final and inevitable doom. But the comic hero must be saved, and when there is no logical exit, in normal human terms, heaven may intervene to rescue him. The novel here touches on the fantastic. "It is, after all," says Eric Rabkin, "fantastic to believe that our fears are all tameable," or that in moments of crisis, when no exit seems possible, the supernatural will intervene to save us.

Good contemporary Palestinian literature is disturbing. It raises questions that shake us because they do not simply relate to the moment and a particular historical "event," but transcend them to probe into problems of injustice, aggression, and coercion as they are imposed on a contemporary human consciousness that is fully aware of their implications. There has never been an age like ours in its global recognition of the possibility for freedom, liberty, and human dignity, and in its determination to defy all forms of aggression. This means that, for aggression to continue, the machine of coercion utilized to repress the inevitable movements of freedom must, perforce, grow constantly more and more "crushing and grinding," more and more deadly. Perhaps *The Pessoptimist*, by demonstrating the various aspects of a particularly grievous situation, can help to show the ultimate absurdity of modern forms of aggression. In this sense, the message of the novel is global.

Salma Khadra Jayyusi

BOOK ONE:
SAEED, THE ILL-FATED
PESSOPTIMIST

So, you men!
And women!
You Sheikhs, Rabbis, Cardinals!
You, nurses, and girls in factories—
How long must you await
The postman with those letters
You so anticipate,
Across the dead-dry barriers?
And you, you men!
And you, women!
Don't wait still more, don't wait!
Now, off with your sleep-clothes
And to yourselves compose
Those letters you so anticipate!

Samīh al-Qāsim

1

One:

Saeed Claims to Have Met Creatures from Outer Space

In his letter to me, Saeed, the ill-fated Pessoptimist, pleaded. "Please tell my story. It is surely as weird as the story of Moses's staff, the resurrection of Jesus, and the election of the husband of a lady bird to the presidency of the United States.

The fact is I've disappeared. But I'm not dead. I wasn't killed at the border, as some of you imagined. Nor did I join the guerrilla movement, as those who knew my virtue feared. Nor am I rotting long-forgotten in some jail, as your friends may suppose.

Now, now! Patience, please! And don't ask, "Who is this 'Saeed' fellow?" Or, "Since he drew no attention throughout his life, why should we give him any now?"

All right. I know my place. I'm not one of your so-called leaders, someone thought worthy of notice by an elite. What I am, my dear sir, is—the office boy!

Didn't you just break up at that Israeli joke about the lion that sneaked inside the offices of the executive committee of the *Histadrut*, the Labor Union Confederation? First day it ate the director of union organization, but not one of his colleagues noticed. Next day it devoured the director of Arab affairs, but the rest didn't miss him.

3

So the lion went on roving happily about, munching contentedly. Finally it ate the office boy, and then they caught it right away.

Yep, I'm that office boy, honored friend. So why didn't you notice I'd gone?

No problem. What matters is that my disappearance, for all its weirdness, was something I'd been expecting all my life. Anyway, the miracle did occur, fine sir, and I did indeed meet with creatures from outer space. I'm in their company right now. As I write to you of my fantastic mystery, I'm soaring with them high above you.

Now don't be a skeptic. Don't say the Age of Miracles is past. What makes you always get things upside down?

By those heavenly hosts with whom I abide, I swear this age has got to be the strangest since the destruction of those errant ancestors of ours, the peoples of Aad and Thamood.[1] But we're used to the wonders of today. Why, if our forebears were to arise and hear the radio, see television, and witness a jumbo jet landing at an airport, spitting and roaring in the pitch-black night, they would think us polytheists for sure.

But we're used to these wonders. We don't raise an eyebrow if kings are deposed or if they stay. Brutus is no big deal now, no subject worth writing about. "Et tu Brute," indeed! The Arabs certainly don't say, "Et tu Baybars"; Qutuz,[2] the sultan this hero Baybars murdered, could only, after all, mutter a grunt in Turkish. And now our great hero Abu Zaid El-Hilaly[3] bends to kiss royal hands. But the sultans have no cause for concern. "I'm no Qutuz," say the kings. And their slaves repeat, "This is no age for Baybars!"[4]

The moon is closer to us now than are the fig trees of our departed village. You accept all these wonders—why not mine too?

Easy there, easy! Don't press me for more details yet. Everything in its own time. Please don't pester me with questions about my companions, how they look, dress, organize, and think. Oh, it all makes me feel so superior! I now know what you don't. Why shouldn't I put on airs?

As for why they chose me alone of all God's creatures—well, I'm not sure I am the only one ever to meet with them. When I asked them what they would think of my informing you of what has happened to me so that the world might know, they just smiled and

4

said: "We have no objection. But the world won't find out. Your friend won't believe you. You see, all that descends from the sky is not necessarily divinely inspired. This itself is one of your 'miracles.' "

So, although I might not be the only one, I most certainly have been chosen by them. And you too, my fine friend, are chosen as well. I have selected you to relate my weirdest wonder of all. You may well puff with pride.

Why did they choose me? Because I chose them. I spent my whole life searching for them, waiting for them, relying on their protection, until meeting them became inevitable.

You find this peculiar? Never mind. In the so-called Age of Ignorance, before Islam, our ancestors used to form their gods from dates and eat them when in need. Who is more ignorant then, dear sir, I or those who ate their gods?

You might say: "It's better for people to eat their gods than for the gods to eat them."

But I'd respond, "Yes, but their gods were made of dates."

Two:

Saeed Reports How His Life in Israel Was All Due to the Munificence of an Ass

Let's start at the beginning. My whole life has been strange, and a strange life can only end strangely. When I asked my extraterrestrial friend why he took me in, he merely replied, "What alternative did you have?"

So when did it all begin?

When I was born again, thanks to an ass.

During the fighting in 1948 they waylaid us and opened fire, shooting my father, may he rest in peace. I escaped because a stray donkey came into the line of fire and they shot it, so it died in place of me. My subsequent life in Israel, then, was really a gift from that unfortunate beast. What value then, honored sir, should we assign to this life of mine?

I consider myself quite remarkable. You've no doubt read of dogs lapping up poisoned water and dying to warn their masters and save their lives. And of horses, too, racing the wind bearing their wounded riders to safety, only to die of exhaustion themselves. But I'm the first man, to my knowledge, to be saved by a mulish donkey, an animal unable either to race the wind or to bark. I truly am remarkable. That must be why the men from outer space chose me.

Tell me, please do, what makes one truly remarkable? Must

one be different from all the rest or, indeed, be very much one of them?

You said you never noticed me before. That's because you lack sensitivity, my good friend. How very often you have seen my name in the leading newspapers. Didn't you read of the hundreds imprisoned by Haifa police when that melon exploded in Hanatir Square, now Paris Square? Afterwards every Arab they found in Lower Haifa, pedestrian or on wheels, they put in jail. The papers published the names of everyone notable who was caught, but merely gave general reference to the rest.

The rest—yes, that's me! The papers haven't ignored me. How can you claim not to have heard of me? I truly am remarkable. For no paper with wide coverage, having sources, resources, advertisements, celebrity writers, and a reputation, can ignore me. Those like me are everywhere—towns, villages, bars, everywhere. I am "the rest." I am remarkable indeed!

Three:

Saeed Gives His Ancestry

Saeed, the ill-fated Pessoptimist—my name fits my appearance precisely. The Pessoptimist family is truly noble and long established in our land. It traces its origins to a Cypriot girl from Aleppo. Tamerlane[5], unable to find room for her head in his pyramid of skulls, for all its reported dimensions of 20,000 arms length by 10 high, sent her with one of his lieutenants to Baghdad, where she was to clean herself up and await his return. But she made a fool of the man. They say, and this is a family secret, that this was the cause of the infamous massacre. Anyway, she ran off with a Bedouin of the Tuwaisat tribe named Abjar, of whom a poet has said:

> *Abjar, Abjar, son of Abjar,*
> *Divorced his wife when he couldn't feed her.*

He divorced her when he found she had deceived him with Loaf, son of Hunger, from the Jaftlick lowlands, who in turn divorced her in Beersheba. Our forefathers went on divorcing our grandmothers until our journey brought us to a flat and fragrant land at the shore of the sea called Acre, then on to Haifa at the other side of the bay. We continued this practice of divorcing our wives right up until the state was founded.

After the first misfortunes, those of 1948, the members of our great family became scattered, living in all of the Arab countries not yet occupied. And so I have relatives working in the very Arabian Aal Rabi court, with posts in the Bureau of Translation—both from and into Persian, I might add. And I have one who has specialized in lighting the cigarettes of different kings. We also had a captain in Syria, a major in Iraq and a lieutenant-colonel in Lebanon. The last mentioned, however, died of a heart attack when the Intra Bank there, the country's biggest, went bankrupt. The first Arab to be appointed by the government of Israel as head of the Committee for Distribution of Dandelion and Watercress in Upper Galilee is from our family, even though his mother, so they say, was a divorced Circassian girl. And he still claims, so far unsuccessfully, distribution rights for Lower Galilee too. My father, may he rest in peace, did many favors for the state before it was founded. These services of his are known in detail by his good friend Adon (Mr., that is) Safsarsheck, the retired police officer.

After my father fell a martyr on the open road and I was redeemed by the ass, my family took the boat to Acre. When we found that we were in no danger, and that everyone was busy saving their skins, we fled to Lebanon to save ours. And there we sold them to live.

When we had nothing left to sell, I recalled my father's behest to me as he breathed his last, there on the open road. "Go," he had said, "to Mr. Safsarsheck[6] and say to him: 'My father, before his martyrdom, sent you his compliments and asked you to fix me up.' "

And fix me he did.

9

Four:

Saeed Enters Israel for the First Time

I crossed the border into Israel in the car of a doctor affiliated with the Arab Salvation Army. He used to flirt with my sister in his clinic in Haifa. When we emigrated to Tyre, in Lebanon, we found him awaiting us. And when I came to suspect what was going on between him and my sister, he began treating me as his dearest friend. Then his wife began to fancy me.

One day, the doctor asked me, "Can you keep a secret?"

I replied, "Like a star over two lovers."

"Then hold your tongue, for my wife won't hold hers."

And so, for my sister's sake, I held mine.

When I revealed to him my desire to sneak into Israel, he promptly volunteered to take me in his car. "It will be better for you to go," he said.

"And for you too," I responded.

"God bless you then," he said.

And my mother did bless us farewell.

We reached Tarshiha just as the sun and the villagers were abandoning it. The Arab guards stopped us. When the doctor showed them his papers, they greeted us warmly. I still felt scared though. But the doctor joked and swore with them, and they laughed and swore back.

In Maaliya we slept. But before dawn I awoke to hear whispering coming from the doctor's bed nearby. I held my breath and made out a woman's voice whispering that her husband would not be awake that early. I told myself that this could not be my sister since she as yet had no husband. So I went contentedly back to sleep.

We lunched at the home of that woman's father in Abu Snan, which was at that time in no-man's-land; that is, it was territory frequented only by spies, cattle merchants, and stray donkeys.

They hired an ass for me and I rode it down to Kufr Yasif. This was in the summer of 1948. And it was riding this donkey as I descended from Abu Snan to Kufr Yasif that I celebrated my twenty-fourth birthday.

They directed me to the headquarters of the military governor. I entered it still riding the donkey. It proudly mounted the three steps at the building's entrance. Soldiers rushed towards me amazed. I shouted, "Safsarsheck, Safsarsheck!"

A fat soldier ran toward me shouting, "I am the military governor, dismount!"

"I am so-and-so, the son of so-and-so," I replied, "and I shall only alight at the door of Mr. Safsarsheck." He swore at me violently but I shouted, "I claim sanctuary with Adon Safsarsheck."

But he merely cursed Mr. Safsarsheck.

So I dismounted from the donkey.

Five:

Research on the Origins of the Pessoptimists

When I alighted from the donkey, I found that I was taller than the military governor. I felt much relieved at being bigger than him without the help of the donkey's legs. So I settled comfortably into a chair in the school they had converted into the governor's headquarters. The blackboards were being used as Ping-Pong tables.

There I sat, at ease, thanking God for making me taller than the military governor without the help of the donkey's legs.

That's the way our family is and why we bear the name Pessoptimist. For this word combines two qualities, pessimism and optimism, that have been blended perfectly in the character of all members of our family since our first divorced mother, the Cypriot. It is said that the first to so name us was Tamerlane, following the second massacre of Baghdad. This was when it was reported to him that my first ancestor, Abjar son of Abjar, mounted on his horse outside the city walls, had stared back at the tongues of flame and shouted, "After me, the deluge!"

Take me, for example. I don't differentiate between optimism and pessimism and am quite at a loss as to which of the two characterizes me. When I awake each morning I thank the Lord he did not take my soul during the night. If harm befalls me during the day, I thank Him that it was no worse. So which am I, a pessimist or an optimist?

12

My mother is also a Pessoptimist. My older brother used to work at the port of Haifa. One day a storm blew up and overturned the crane he was operating, throwing them both onto the rocks and down into the sea. They collected his remains and brought them to us. Neither his head nor his insides could be found. He had been married less than a month and his bride sat weeping and bewailing her hard luck. My mother sat there too, crying silently.

Suddenly my mother became agitated and started beating her hands together. She said hoarsely: "It's best it happened like this and not some other way!"

None of us was surprised at her conclusion except the bride, who was not from our family and therefore did not understand our kind of wisdom. She almost lost her mind and began screaming in my mother's face, "What do you mean, 'some other way'? You ill-fated [this, of course, was the name of my father, may he rest in peace] hag! What worse way could there have been?"

My mother did not appreciate this childish outburst and answered with all the calm assurance of a fortuneteller: "For you to have run off during his life, my girl, to have run away with some other man." One should remember, of course, that my mother knew our family history all too well.

My brother's widow did indeed run off with another man two years later and he turned out to be sterile. When my mother heard that he was so, she repeated her favorite saying, "And why should we not praise God?"

So what are we then? Optimists or pessimists?

Six:

How Saeed First Participated in the War of Independence

Now let's return, my dear sir, to the headquarters of the military governor and how, as soon as he cursed Adon Safsarsheck I alighted from the donkey. It became clear to me very soon indeed that in cursing a person one is sometimes really expressing jealousy rather than contempt.

As soon as I seated myself in the chair, cheered by the thought that I was taller than the military governor even without the donkey's legs, he hurried to the telephone and gabbled some words of which I could only distinguish two, namely, *ill-fated* and *Safsarsheck*, both names to be associated with me for a long time. When finished, he threw down the receiver and screamed in my face to get up. I did so.

"I am Abu Isaac. Follow me," he ordered. So I followed him to a jeep parked near the entrance. My donkey was standing beside it, sniffing.

"Let's go," said Abu Isaac. He climbed into his jeep and I mounted my donkey. But he shrieked in fury, and my donkey and I so shook with fear that I fell from its back and found myself in the car next to the military governor. It proceeded westward along a dirt road flanked by stalks of sesame.

"Where to?" I asked.

14

"Acre. And shut up!" he replied.

So shut up I did. After continuing for a few minutes he brought the jeep to a sudden halt and jumped from it like a shot, his gun in his hand. He raced into the sesame stalks, parting them with his paunch. I saw a peasant woman crouching down there, in her lap a child, its eyes wide in terror.

"From which village?" demanded the governor.

The mother remained crouching, staring at him askance, although he stood right over her, huge as a mountain.

"From Berwah?" he yelled.

She made no response but continued to stare at him.

He then pointed his gun straight at the child's head and screamed, "Reply, or I'll empty this into him!"

At this I tensed, ready to spring at him come what may. After all, the blood of youth surged hot within me, at my age then of twenty-four. And not even a stone could have been unmoved at this sight. However, I recalled my father's final counsel and my mother's blessing and then said to myself, "I certainly shall attack him if he fires his gun. But so far he is merely threatening her." I remained at the ready.

The woman did reply, "Yes, from Berwah."

"Are you returning there?" he demanded.

"Yes, returning."

"Didn't we warn you," he yelled, "that anyone returning there will be killed? Don't you all understand the meaning of discipline? Do you think it's the same as chaos? Get up and run ahead of me. Go back anywhere you like to the east. And if I ever see you again on this road I'll show you no mercy."

The woman stood up and, gripping her child by the hand, set off toward the east, not once looking back. Her child walked beside her, and he too never looked back.

At this point I observed the first example of that amazing phenomenon that was to occur again and again until I finally met my friends from outer space. For the further the woman and child went from where we were, the governor standing and I in the jeep, the taller they grew. By the time they merged with their own shadows in the sinking sun they had become bigger than the plain of Acre itself. The governor still stood there awaiting their final disappearance, while I remained huddled in the jeep. Finally he asked in amazement, "Will they never disappear?"

This question, however, was not directed at me.

Berwah is the village of the poet Mahmoud Darwish, who said fifteen years later:

I laud the executioner, victor over a made-up eye;
Hurrah for the vanquisher of villages, hurrah for the butcher of
* infants.*

Was he this very child? Had he gone on walking eastward after releasing himself from his mother's hand, leaving her in the shadows?

Now why am I, my good sir, relating this trivial incident to you? For many reasons. And among them is this phenomenon of bodies growing ever larger the farther they move from our sight.

Another reason is that this incident provides further proof that the name of our ancient family inspires respect in the hearts of the authorities of the state of Israel. For were it not for this respect, the governor would most certainly have emptied his gun into my head when he saw me tense up, in readiness to attack him.

Yet another reason is that I felt for the first time that I was fulfilling the mission of my father, may he rest in peace, and serving the state, even if only after its establishment. So I thought to myself, Why should I not be on familiar terms with the military governor?

I therefore took the liberty to blurt out: "Er, this vehicle of yours, what make is it?"

"Shut up!" he replied. And I did.

It was that same poet of Berwah mentioned above who later said:

We know best about those devils
Who of children prophets make.

He realized only quite recently that those same devils could also render a whole nation utterly and completely forgotten.

16

Seven:

Yuaad's[7] Name Is Mentioned for the First Time

Acre, its night pitch black as an Abbasid flag, welcomed our entry. I remembered my girl friend Yuaad, who never smiled to anyone but me on the train. My heart beat fast.

Acre was my secondary school, and Yuaad my primary love.

For Acre, which had resisted the Crusaders longer than any other city and had later rebuffed Napoleon, and had not in the interim been conquered by the Mongols, still maintained its dignity with age, even though its walls were now a rendezvous for hashish smokers and its lighthouse glimmered faintly, like Khodja's lamp. It continued to be the metropolis even after Haifa had become industrialized and vigorous.

Acre's secondary school, its thick-walled rooms on the shoulder of the eastern wall, was still academically superior to the one in Haifa. We were thus enrolled in the *firqa* ("barracks") school, and we commuted daily by train from Haifa. It was on the train that I met Yuaad, also from Haifa. She attended the girls' school in Acre and she used to hug her satchel and commute with us. But she used to sit quite alone in the only closed compartment on the train. She always went straight into that compartment with her veil in place and she would be wearing it when she came out. But through the crack in the door of her compartment she would exchange secret

17

glances with me, with those fine green eyes of hers. I fell head over heels in love with her.

One morning she called me over and asked me to explain an English word to her. When I could not, she told me the meaning herself and asked me to sit down. From then on I would sit with her on both trips. My, how I loved her! She said that she loved me, too, because I was entertaining and had a hearty laugh.

The jealousy of one of my classmates caused me much silent pain. He reported me to the principal of her school, who sent a letter to our principal. The latter summoned all the students who commuted by train from Haifa and ranted and raged. "Between Haifa and Acre, I tell you, between Haifa and Acre, there's a sea, a sea! This has always been a conservative city, ever since the days of Saladin."[8]

I recalled the famous traveler Ibn Jubair,[9] who spent two nights at an inn in Acre during Saladin's time and wrote, "The town seethes with heresy and blasphemy," and "it is full of vice and sin." The father of my own father, may they both rest in peace, whose wife ran off with another man, used to tell us when we were young that "she did that because she was from Accaaaaaaa," stretching the last vowel of the town's Arabic pronunciation for emphasis.

So I looked the principal straight in the face and shouted, in something of a whisper, "But *she* is not from Acre!"

He expelled me from his office and reported the matter to her family. They sent someone to beat me up in the station, and that made me love her even more. I attacked the classmate who had reported us, and we fell from the train onto the sands at the beach. Unharmed, we walked back to Haifa together after bathing in the sea. On the way some Bedouins gave us paper-thin bread with salt and oil to eat, and then they stole our satchels. As a result, that boy became one of my best friends. He still is.

Yuaad was never on the train after the principal wrote to her parents. But I remained smitten with love for her.

The governor and I entered the police building on the western shore, and he handed me over to one of the officers. The latter ordered me to return next morning for transfer to Haifa. Then he considered the situation and asked, "But where will you spend the night?"

"Yuaad," I replied. The officer, demanding to know whether I was deaf, repeated his question.

I replied that the only person I knew in Acre was the principal of the school.

The officer then consulted with the governor, who told him to take me to the Jazzar mosque. We set off in his jeep. When we arrived at the drinking fountain near its gate, he stopped the car and we alighted. He drummed the ancient door-knocker on the gate of the mosque. A sudden din arose; then there was total silence. An infant began to cry but was soon hushed. Next we heard the dragging of feet, and the gate was opened by an emaciated old man in tattered clothes. He welcomed us effusively.

The officer told him, "This is another man who must report to the police station tomorrow morning."

"Come in, my son," the old man invited me, and I entered.

When I saw his face I recognized my old principal and exclaimed, "Oh, teacher. My father, may he rest in peace, commended me to your beneficence."

"My beneficence is very extensive, my boy," he responded. "Come and see for yourself."

Eight:

A Strange Evening Spent in the Courtyard of the Jazzar Mosque

My one-time teacher clapped his hands three times and addressed the dark shadows of the courtyard: "Continue whatever you were doing, folks. He's one of us."

Immediately a great hubbub arose and hands were removed from the mouths of little children. I watched as figures approached from inside the Ahmady mosque school, which encircled the courtyard on its three sides, to the east, north, and west. People crowded all around us and, after greeting me warmly and profusely, sat cross-legged on the ground and asked who I was.

I told them I had just returned from Lebanon. What a flurry of excitement that caused!

My teacher shouted, "Now there's one of our boys for you, folks! And if he can come back, why, the others certainly can too."

Someone asked, "Did you cross in secret?"

Now I didn't want to explain to them about my sister's lover, the doctor, nor about the donkey, nor about Adon Safsarsheck, and so answered, "Yes."

"Oh, then they'll deport you tonight," they said.

"But my father, now deceased, was friends with one of their officials, a man named Adon Safsarsheck," I informed them indignantly.

Again a sudden din, this time of anger, arose, and my
did his best to reassure them. "He's still only a boy," he i
in spite of the fact was that I was twenty-four that night. I inwardly
thanked my teacher for not pretending that I was a young woman
to save me from their anger, which I found completely inexplicable.
Cooled down at last, they began to accept me and bombarded me
with questions about their relatives who had taken refuge in Lebanon.

"We're from Kwaykaat.[10] They demolished it and evicted everyone. Did you meet anyone from Kwaykaat?"

I was much tickled at the repetition of the *k* in Kwaykaat but
managed to suppress my laughter.

Then a woman's voice rising from behind the sundial over to
the west saved the situation. We heard her say, "The girl isn't
sleeping, Shukriyya; she's dead." There was a stifled scream and
everyone caught their breath until it stopped. Then they continued
their questioning.

I answered that I had met no one from Kwaykaat.

"I am from al-Manshiyya. There's not a stone left standing
there except the tombs. Did you meet anyone from al-Manshiyya?"

"No."

"We are from Amqa. They plowed all its houses under and
spilled its oil onto the ground. Did you meet anyone from Amqa?"

"No."

"We over here are from Berwah. They forced us out and ob-
literated it. Did you meet anyone from Berwah?"

"I did see one woman from there hiding with her child among
the sesame stalks."

I heard many voices trying to guess who this woman was, and
they ennumerated more than twenty mothers. Finally one old man
shouted: "That's enough. She is Mother Berwah. Stop guessing.
God is her only refuge and ours."

And they did stop guessing. But soon voices erupted again,
persisting in drawing out their relationships to their villages, all of
which I understood to have been razed by the army:

"We are from Ruwais." "We are from al-Hadatha." "We are
from el-Damun."

"We are from Mazraa." "We are from Shaab." "We are from Miy'ār."

"We are from Waarat el-Sarris." "We are from al-Zeeb." "We are from el-Bassa."

"We are from el-Kabri." "We are from Iqrit." "We are from Kufr Bir'im."

"We are from Dair el-Qasi." "We are from Saasaa." "We are from el-Ghābisiy."

"We are from Suhmata." "We are from al-Safsaf." "We are from Kufr 'Inān."

Please do not expect me, my dear sir, after all this time, to remember the names of all the villages laid waste to which these figures made claim that evening in the courtyard of the Jazzar mosque. We of Haifa used to know more about the villages of Scotland than we did about those of Galilee. Most of these villages I have never heard mentioned except for that one evening.

Yes, don't blame me, my very fine sir. Blame your friends. And did not your poet of Galilee, Tawfiq Zayyad, write:

I shall carve the name of every stolen plot
And where my village boundaries lay;
What homes exploded,
What trees uprooted, what tiny wild flowers crushed.
All this to remember. And I'll keep on carving
Each act of this my tragedy, each phase of the catastrophe,
All things, minor and major,
On an olive tree in the courtyard of my home.

How long must he continue carving? How soon will these years of oblivion pass, effacing all our memories? When will the words carved on the olive tree be read? And are there any olives left in courtyards still?

When they failed to receive satisfactory answers from me and realized that my acquaintance was limited to that of my own family, my teacher, and Adon Safsarsheck, they dispersed into their various corners, leaving me alone with my one-time principal.

Nine:

The First Signal from Outer Space

When the gathering broke up I remained there alone with my teacher. Gratitude welled within me for being rescued from the anger of those ghostlike figures, and I had a strong urge to express it. This man, you will remember, was the one who had destroyed my relationship with the green-eyed Yuaad. But I am a big-hearted fellow and I told him how very happy I was to spend my first night in this new state in his care. He had been recommended to me by my father as second only to Adon Safsarsheck. "What are you doing here, principal?" I asked.

"I reunite families," he replied. Then he added: "The truth is, son, that they are no worse than others like them in history."

I nodded. approvingly and he continued: "It's true, they did demolish those villages the others mentioned and did evict their inhabitants. But, my son, they're far more merciful than the conquerors our forefathers had years before.

"Take Acre, for example. When the Crusaders conquered it after a three-week siege in 1104, they slaughtered the people wholesale and confiscated their property. And Acre remained in their hands for eighty-three years, until Saladin freed it after the battle of Hittin, the history of which I taught you in school.

"Then the Crusaders besieged it again for two years, from August 1189 to July 1191, when hunger forced its people to surrender on very harsh terms. When they were unable to meet those terms, the king of the Crusaders, Richard the Lionhearted, ordered the heads of 2,600 hostages to be chopped off. So Acre remained in their hands for another century, one hundred years, my son, until it was liberated by the Mamluk leader Qalawun,[11] in 1291. His military title was al-Alfi, meaning "the Thousander," this rank was, of course, awarded in recognition of the high price paid for him when he was still a slave—one thousand dinars, that is."

I wanted to prove to him that I was still the same clever fellow I had been as a student, and so I asked, "Is the rank of Alluf for the Israeli generals derived from Qalawun's title?"

"God forbid, my son. No. That is derived from the word for a leader of a thousand men, a term used in the Bible. Oh, no! These aren't Mamluks or Crusaders. These are people returning to their country after an absence of two thousand years."

"My, what prodigious memories they have!"

"Anyway, my son, people have been talking for two thousand years in terms of thousands—generals of a thousand men, men slain by the thousands, and so on.

"There is nothing on earth more holy than human blood. That is why our country is called the Holy Land."

"And is my city, Haifa, holy?"

"Every spot of our land has been made holy by the blood of the slain and will go on being made holy, my son. Your city, Haifa, is no different. You see, after the Crusaders conquered Jerusalem, God give it peace, in the year 1099 (and their king, Gottfried, wrote to the Pope boasting that 'heaps of skulls and limbs are to be seen in all the streets and squares of the city,' and that in the Mosque of Omar, God praise him, and where the Muslims took refuge, 'blood reached up to the knees of the horses'). They went on and conquered Haifa too, following a month-long siege by the Venetian fleet. They butchered its inhabitants to the last soul—men, women, and children.

"So Haifa, you see my boy, is not a new city. The point is that after every massacre there was no one left to tell the new generation about their origins."

"But why didn't you teach us about all this holiness, sir?"

"Well, the British do have the right to boast about their own history, you know, especially about that great king of theirs, Richard the Lionhearted. But even without our teaching you all this, they were participating in the process of rendering our country holy by spilling our blood. Conquerors, my son, consider as true history only what they have themselves fabricated."

"Will we be permitted to study this history after the conquerors have left and the country obtains its independence?"

"You'll have to wait and see."

"Will they enter the Jazzar mosque just as the Crusaders did the Mosque of Omar?"

"God forbid! Certainly not! They will simply knock at the door and we will come out to them. They will not defile the sanctity of places of worship; they have plenty of room on the outside."

No sooner had my teacher finished his reassuring comments than we heard loud knocking at the door. "They have arrived," he said.

"Perhaps Adon Safsarsheck has come from Haifa to ask after me," I wondered aloud. But my teacher had already reached the gate. The ghostly figures had already awakened and had begun roaming aimlessly in the courtyard.

We held our breath as we heard that the army had decided to return those refugees who had sought sanctuary in the mosque to their villages of origin at once.

A figure next to me whispered, "Why don't they wait until morning?"

His question astonished me. I could only repeat the maxim: "Charity is best when quickest."

Then someone shouted: "Saeed the Ill-fated alone is to remain with the principal; all the rest must come outside."

I now realized how true my old teacher's comments about them were; they were indeed no worse than King Richard the Lionhearted.

Shukriyya, the woman whose daughter had died, slipped out the eastern gate, carrying the girl's body in her arms. Before she disappeared in the dark marketplace, I asked her, "Where are you going?"

"In the morning I shall bury her here in Acre and then go on my way."

Others slipped out by the southern gate, losing themselves in the old alleys of the town. I asked them why and they replied: "We don't have an Adon Safsarsheck. Those who razed our villages are not going to take us back there."

The remainder of the villagers carried their tattered belongings and their children out the great northern gate. They were put on big trucks which carried them, as my teacher told me later, to the northern borders. There the trucks dumped them and then returned.

After the villagers were gone my teacher came over to me and leaned, as I was doing, against the sundial. I felt quite relaxed, free from all worry. He told me to go and get some sleep, since he had told me all he knew.

But I did not sleep.

For it was that night, as the false dawn broke, that I saw the first signal from outer space.

Ten:

Saeed Reveals a Strange Family Secret

I remained sleepless, not because I was upset, but because I was dazzled by my own good fortune. For here I was, having safely managed to return to my own country. In contrast, the rest of my nation was out there wandering aimlessly, lost and destitute. And those refusing to wander were evicted by force.

All except me! I had sneaked back in the car of a doctor, my sister's lover, and her honor had been saved by the grace of our host's wife in Maaliya. I had then moved from car to donkey, donkey to jeep. And en route to Acre I had been rescued from sure death by my own timely prudence. I had then found sanctuary in the Jazzar mosque under the care of my old teacher, whom I had forgiven. Soldiers had soon removed the ghostly figures and their children, leaving only myself. How could I not feel this night to be my own very special night of good fortune?

Adon Safsarsheck clearly could not be the cause of this great luck. Was he, after all, a magic ring? Or Aladdin's lamp? Some supernatural power had to be at work here.

So I decided to leave the mosque, to discover what the secret was. But before I tell you what occurred when I did go out, I must acquaint you with another attribute of our ancient family quite apart from our pessoptimism and the fact that we're great divorcers.

My father, when martyred, was searching the ground at his feet and so did not detect the ambush. His own father had been struck on the head and killed by a millstone when *he* was searching the ground at his feet. This, then, is a family characteristic: to be looking always for money that some passerby has dropped, hoping always we might discover some treasure that might transform the regular pattern of a monotonous life.

You may be sure, dear sir, that every single old woman in the Arab world whose head precedes her body to the grave and who walks bent over like a number seven is related to us. Similarly all those young men who use every trick conceivable to hear each news-broadcast, never missing one, like fishermen casting their hooks in hope of catching the golden fish, are our close relatives.

But you should not conclude from this that our ancestors always ended up with broken heads. We have found a great amount of lost money, though this has not changed any of the drudgery of our lives.

One of the family's secrets is that, during the days when the Ottomans were leaving and the British entering, my great uncle left his home in the village of———(we are like Freemasons, and do not divulge such details). While he was gazing downward, as is our habit, his head knocked against a stone in a ruined house, and, since his skull was very hard, the stone rolled out of its place. He discovered there before him a shaft with some stairs; he descended them and found himself in a cavelike darkness. An idea sparked, so he lit his lamp, and saw in its light some marble tombs. These he opened and found skulls, remnants of skeletons, and some golden sovereigns which he promptly tucked into the pockets of his baggy trousers. Finally he opened one tomb larger than the rest. In it he found, along with a skull which was, it is said, smaller than the others, a statue of pure gold of Mango Khan,[12] the oldest of Hulaku's[13] brothers, who died of dysentery while campaigning against China. His huge body had been carried to the capital city on two donkeys. They had not yet discovered Boy Scout troops. Nor did they have schools then, so that they could line up students on both sides of the street as they did with us in the thirties in Haifa when they lined us up along Nazareth Street where later the statue of

Faisal I stood, to participate in that king's funeral; he had died in Switzerland, but not of dysentery.[14]

The Mongols decided to kill everyone the funeral met on its way, out of respect for the first Khan, just as we killed three days of study in the thirties in mourning for Faisal I. According to the historians, they killed twenty thousand souls on his funeral march and then one more, that of my great uncle, who expired as he held the statue of Mango Khan seven centuries later.

My great uncle realized, when down at the bottom, that he had at last found the treasure, the one the family had been seeking for many generations. He was so overcome with joy that he dropped his lamp and could not find the door. He began calling out for his wife, estimating that his own house, next door to the ruin, must be directly above him. He told her the story I have just related. He made her solemnly swear not to tell anyone, not even his own brother, but to come down herself through the opening in the wall of the ruined building. She went outside but couldn't find a single ruined house in the village. So she returned home and put her forehead to the ground and shouted down to him. He swore at her for her rashness and ordered her to hold her tongue till morning, when he would find the way out by himself.

When he did not return she told his relatives and they searched but could find no ruins. They, moreover, did not want to tell the authorities, for the officials would only grab the treasure for themselves. So they continued searching for him and Mango's statue until the state was founded. As for his wife, she did not die before she found another husband, one who was not sterile.

As a child, I decided not to die with a bent back like my forebears and so have never searched for treasure at my feet. I began, instead, looking for treasure above, in the endless reaches of space, in this "shoreless sea," as the mystic poet Ibn Arabi[15] described it.

Fate had granted us, when we were in elementary school, one God-damned teacher who was mad about astronomy. He told us all about Abbas Ibn Firnas[16] and Jules Verne and expressed a fanatical pride in all the old Arab astronomers; from Averroes[17], who first studied sun spots, to al-Batani al-Harrani,[18] who first deduced that the time equation changes slowly over the generations and who first accurately computed the length of the solar year. Our accursed teacher once announced that while the sun year's actual length is 365 days, 5 hours, 48 minutes and 46 seconds, al-Batani calculated it to be 365 days, 5 hours, 46 minutes and 32 seconds, a difference of 2 minutes and 4 seconds. The Arabs, that miserable teacher of ours concluded, always did things quicker then—they thought faster than the earth moved around the sun—whereas they have now surrendered their power of thought to others.

This infernal teacher used to keep us in class after school, close the windows, and tell us proudly of the scientist al-Biruni,[19] who had discovered that the earth was round and, some eight hundred years before Newton, that all bodies were attracted to it. He used to gabble constantly about al-Hasan ibn al-Haytham,[20] who was—and here the fellow would lower his voice to a conspiratorial whisper—the first to develop today's scientific methodology which requires deductions based only on observation of concrete reality and reasoning by analogy. For the Arabs, so said this accursed teacher, would first act and then dream, not as they do now—first dream and then continue to dream.

I dreamed that history would remember me as it had our ancient astronomers. This dream of mine survived right up to the time they ambushed my father, may his soul rest in peace, and established the state of Israel.

This same miserable man used to assure us that the Arabs were the first to use zero as we use it now. Then they divided one by zero and proved to us that outer space is limitless and that the universe in it, as Ibn Arabi wrote; "swims in a shoreless sea, in the jet black of eternity."

There must certainly be worlds other than ours, and better too. No doubt they'll find us before we them. Well, the Turks left and the British came to us without that teacher wavering in his theories; so how can I doubt them—I, a young man whose whole life is still before him, the British having left and Israel come in?

Yes, ever since that time I began looking upward and awaiting their arrival. Either they will transform my monotonous and boring life completely, or they can take me away with them.

Is there an alternative?

That's why I left the Jazzar mosque at the hour of false dawn and roamed the dark streets of Acre, gazing upward all the time.

Eleven:

Saeed Remembers How He Did Not Die a Martyr in a Valley at the Lebanese Border

Since I had no fears regarding my safety and was certain that the worst would not befall me, I strolled down the stairs of the northern gate, filled a bowl with water at the drinking fountain, drank my fill, said a prayer for the soul of Ahmad al-Jazzar, and went on my way.

The broad road to the north, to Ras al-Naqura and then to Lebanon, stretched before me. Seeing it, I immediately remembered Ghazala. I lowered my head in shame and turned around and walked away.

There had been three of us young men, all classmates. When the general strike of 1939 was over, we decided to cross into Lebanon to visit the headquarters of the Arab resistance there and to ask for arms. We hired a car that took us near Ras al-Naqura. There we alighted and moved off on foot to the right, through the vineyards. We descended a gorge and the sky seemed to darken. By the time we began climbing the hill on the other side, we were exhausted and burned with thirst. My friends urged me to continue, but I began to cry. They finally left me behind after letting me choose between continuing the climb with them or dying a martyr, alone. I chose the former, but every time I caught up with them, they had already satisfied their thirst with rich grapes. I began to quench mine like them, but they did not wait for me.

Suddenly there appeared a girl of about my age who called out to her father, "Here's a young hero from Palestine!" The farmer replied that she should give me food and drink. As she and I exchanged words I fell in love with her. She told me her name was Ghazala,[21] and that I was her own gazelle, for girls found me irresistible.

I promised her I would visit her again the following week, when I would be returning with weapons and ammunition, and that I would meet her under that same vine. She replied that she would tell her father, for he would never refuse her engagement to a nice young man from Palestine.

I bent over to kiss her, but she veered away like a gazelle, laughing. "Make sure you come back from Beirut first." I did not comprehend the reason for her elusiveness, but I had no time to linger. I had to hurry to catch up with my friends.

I found them standing on the main road, surrounded by several Lebanese border guards. I said to myself, "It's good I dropped behind and fell in love with Ghazala."

The police took them aside to the left, then to a camp on the shore, where they were lost from view. Taking the same road, but in the opposite direction, they did not notice me. I was pleased to be safe but wondered where I could go since I had no money and no address to go to. How would I get by in Beirut?

Telling myself that my situation was worse than prison, I realized that I had to return to my friends. Prison would not be as bad.

As I joined them the officer asked, "And who might you be?"

"The third of them," I replied.

"Why on earth are you giving yourself up?"

"Well, I have no money and nowhere to go."

"Where's your money?" he asked.

"The oldest of us has it," we replied.

We had managed to scrape together twenty pounds. Of this the police took ten, cursed us, and gave the rest to our senior partner. We spent the money in the red-light district of Beirut and then set off for home. This time we did not bother to turn off the road into the vineyards, for the ten pound bribe covered both crossings. When the officer met us on our return trip he asked, "Where are your weapons, my gallant warriors?"

The oldest of us replied, "Our weapon is knowledge, and we're quite penniless."

The officer hit the oldest on his behind and shouted, "Cross on over!"

We fled toward our border while the oldest of us remarked, "Well, to know something is better than not to know it."

"It's good it happened like this and not some other way," I said. The others slapped me and I cried.

But I was really weeping for Ghazala, whose gazelle had lost his soul in Beirut. I now understood why she had not let me kiss her.

Later on, as a refugee in Tyre, I kept longing to visit the vineyards on the borders, right up until the day I heard the doctor, my sister's lover, say, "The Palestinians have become refugees, and girls now shun them." After that I turned my attention to refugee girls. Refugee girls, I thought, are for refugee boys. But I found them, unlike us boys, to be much in demand, having no time for us.

So I returned to the state of Israel, feeling very thirsty.

Twelve:

How the True Dawn Saves Saeed from Getting Lost in the Subterranean Tunnels of Acre

And so, my respectable friend, that is why I turned to the left off the Beirut road and entered the slums of Acre. I walked around the mosque until I arrived at the Kharaba quarter. The false dawn disappeared and the night became very dark. I stumbled along, feeling my way, until I noticed a light to the west, out toward the sea, winking at me rhythmically as if to invite me there.

That light reminded me of my old Arabic teacher whose left eye had a twitch. When I first saw it winking I thought he was calling me to the blackboard, and so I walked to the front of the class. The teacher yelled, "Back to your place, you idiot!" And I retreated.

But his left eye kept on winking at me. At last I thought I understood what he meant. When he began singing to us the anthem, "Palestine Is My Country, So Come All My Children," and winked with his left eye, I burst out laughing before he had time to finish one verse. Stunned, he came to an abrupt stop. I could hear my apprehensive classmates quicken their breathing. Suddenly he went after me with the blackboard pointer and shattered it completely. He ordered me to stay after school and copy twenty times the following verses from the pre-Islamic poet-prince Imru al-Qais:[22]

My friend wept to see the road ahead
And realized that it to Caesar led;
I told him, "Allow not your eyes to weep, for we
Our kingdom back must get or die and pardoned be."

Twenty times, mind you! Ever since that occasion I have fully realized the consequences of sarcasm and have been grateful for that twitch in my teacher's eye. It was good for me that he broke his pointer hitting me.

But clearly this light now winking in the west could not be from my teacher's left eye. For the ghostly figures in the mosque had told me how he had fallen a martyr, God have mercy on him, while transporting explosives from Haifa to Acre the same week that the British army had exterminated the "rebels" in the battle of Musrara at Jerusalem and at Qastal on the slopes of the city. That was just before the Arab legion under Abu Hunaik, Glubb Pasha[23] that is, marched against those regions of Palestine after it had been decided to render them empty of Arabs.

And so I advanced toward the winking light, confident that it was a call from heaven. But as I approached the sea, I discovered that it was only Acre's lighthouse, to my left, that was beckoning to me.

This one light, nevertheless, did thrill me, since all others had been turned off in our shy and stoic city. I advanced toward the lighthouse, the road empty and the sea calm. The tide was ebbing and the only motion came as the waves caressed the rocks crouching there before the wall, ready to catch another Napoleonic hat.[24]

Yes indeed, my dear sir. If human beings persist in crouching motionless, why should the rocks of Acre not do likewise? The people of Acre had always repeated disdainfully: "Why should Acre fear the roaring of the sea?" But then their neighbors, the people of Haifa, proved to them as they raced to them in flight across the stormy waters that they had even less fear of the sea than the folk of Acre.

Suddenly I heard a voice calling to me, "Saeed! Saeed"! I felt like a man peeping through a keyhole at a virgin in her chamber.

I was embarrassed and wanted to retreat, but the voice urged me forward. I said, "Here I am."

"Come nearer," it replied.

I saw the figure of a man emerging from the rocks of the light-house as the light shone toward me and then disappearing as it receded. He was wrapped in a blue cloak flecked with white foam, like the lighthouse itself. As he approached I walked toward him; we met in the middle of the open space between one end of the sea wall to the right and the other end to the left, in the Fakhura quarter.

His face was mostly hidden, but I did see wrinkles like those on the surface of the sea when the east wind blows. I had the strange feeling that there was as much beauty in his wrinkles as there is in the bloom of youth. Had it not been such a dark and scary night I would have bent forward and kissed his cheek.

His eyes too I saw. Large and profound, they seemed to increase in depth as the dark fell on them, then to resurface as the lighthouse beam caught them again, as if symbolizing in rapid sequence the constant recurrence of night and day.

I saw also that his forehead was remarkably broad, far wider than my eyes had detected at first glance. Years later, when I stood before what I thought was just a tall building, and then raised my eyes to find the building was a skyscraper—the first one I had ever seen—and so huge that I could not see all of it, I remembered the brow of that old man of the lighthouse.

He offered me his hand. I shook it and felt so at peace that I left my hand in his. There was some magic in that man's palm, I sensed.

"Were you not looking for me?" he asked.

"All my life, reverend. Have you come at last?"

"We are always here, right here, waiting for you to come to us."

"And to think," I said, my hand still in his, "I used to consider shaking hands a barbaric custom!"

He smiled, his cheek clearing those wavelike wrinkles, as he replied, "We thought that when you adopted this habit, you had crossed halfway to us. We regarded as the very first prophet the man who began hand clapping as a sign of approval; we carved his name on the tablet of the immortals before all others. We feel ashamed that most of you are still too mean to pay that price to an artist or performer. Yes, we've honored two other names before all others on this earth—that of the first to kindle fire and that of the first to shake his brother's hand. Keep yours in mine and be at peace."

Then he asked me, "What is it you want, Saeed?"

"I want you to save me!" I exclaimed.

"From whom?"

Suddenly afraid, I withdrew my hand and held my tongue before it slipped and got me into trouble. My father, may he rest in peace, taught us that people eat one another and that we should therefore trust no one but should suspect all, even our own brothers born to our own mothers and fathers. Even if others did not actually eat you, they could if they wished. My father, may he rest in peace, kept on eating others until they finally did the same to him.

So, prudently, I held my tongue, telling myself that the military governor might well have sent him to test me. I responded, congratulating myself for my alertness: "Well, thanks for your interest, reverend, but I hardly know you."

"Follow me," he then commanded. I thought he might still be testing me and so I followed him. He led me through an arch on the right of the prison, into the courtyard of the Ramal mosque; then we circled the Jazzar mosque until we suddenly came to a passageway leading underground. We followed this and found ourselves in the catacombs of Acre. The light from his eyes glowed to show the way.

Soon we entered a cool and spacious hall with seating along its side walls. We sat down and he observed: "Your ancestors built above their predecessors, but then the age of the archaeologists arrived. They began digging beneath while demolishing above. If you continue like this, you'll reach the dinosaurs."

"What is this place, reverend?" I asked.

"This is the lobby of the merchants of Genoa. They used to sleep here and exchange goods, commit debauchery and gamble, give birth and get born, bury others and be buried."

"Why did they so fill the earth with these tunnels, reverend?"

"To free themselves from worry about those above."

"But the tunnels did not save them!"

"They didn't realize that."

"What is your name, reverend?" I finally asked.

As he gazed at me, I could see two Saeeds looking back at me in wonder: one insistent, the other scared. Smiling, he replied, "Among you, each person bears his own name. But we have whatever name you think appropriate. You may call me the Mahdi, as your ancestors did, or The Imam, or The Savior."

"Do save us, reverend," insisted one Saeed, while the other diminished and shrank.

He stared hard at me, waves of anger in his eyes breaking over both Saeeds, who now vanished. Then he said, "That is the way you always are. When you can no longer endure your misery, yet you cannot bear to pay the high price you know is needed to change it, you come to me for help. But I see what other people do and the price they pay, allowing no one to squeeze them into one of these tunnels, and then I become furious with you. What is it you lack? Is any one of you lacking a life he can offer, or lacking a death to make him fear for his life?"

I felt stunned, absolutely breathless, as I listened. The tunnel swam before my eyes. Then I remembered the promised dawn in my beloved city of Haifa. My sense of foreboding grew stronger. I explained to him, "Tomorrow, reverend, I shall return to my city of Haifa and live there. So please give me advice."

He grew calmer and replied, "My advice will not help you. However, I will tell you a story I heard, set in Persia, about an axe without a handle that was thrown among some trees.

"The trees said to each other, 'This has not been thrown here for any good reason.'

"But one perfectly ordinary tree observed: 'Provided none of you supply a stick for its arse, you have nothing to fear from it.'

"You'd better go now; this story's not fit to repeat."

"May I see you again, reverend?"

"Whenever you want. Just come down to these tunnels."

"At what time, reverend?"

"When you feel completely drained of strength."

"When?"

But he had disappeared. And I remained alone, wandering from one tunnel to another. Finally the true dawn emerged, splitting open the womb of the earth, and I found myself in the courtyard of the mosque, yawning and stretching my limbs.

Thirteen:

How Saeed Becomes a Leader in the Union of Palestinian Workers

Now that I have so much free time I often wonder, recalling my first meeting with that strange man from outer space, why it was that I let him go without grabbing his hem and insisting that he save me from this terrible life.

But at the time I was busy preparing myself for the meeting with Adon Safsarsheck, a man who was very close to my heart, like my grandmother's good luck charm.

I won't bore you with unnecessary details, illustrious sir. I entered the police station in Acre at precisely 7:30 that morning, as ordered. I asked after his honor, the military governor, who was to take me to Haifa. They made me wait till four o'clock in the afternoon without food or drink except one cup of tea from a young soldier who spoke to me in English and whom I answered even more fluently in the same language.

He told me that he was a volunteer who had come to fight feudalism, and that he loved the Arabs. Before I left the station, he came over and shook hands with me warmly and promised that, when the war was over, they would build us kibbutzim. They would depend heavily on "liberal" young men like myself who knew a civilized language well. He said, "Shalom," and I answered "Peace," showing how civilized I was. He laughed and said, "Salaam, salaam," the Arabic word, and my depression was quite alleviated.

Then a soldier put me between himself and the driver in a dusty, muddy army vehicle, and we rode in silence. Soon we were approaching Haifa, the wild plain called "happiness." It was useless to search out the anemones that once filled that plain because, I realized, there was no room for the memories of childhood cramped in that narrow seat scarcely large enough for the three of us.

"Welcome to the Medinah of Israel," said the truck driver.

This made me think they had changed the name of my beloved city, Haifa, to the Medinah of Israel and I felt depressed, just as I did later when we passed the Valley of the Cross and found it empty both of people and of that din of bullets we had known so well in the last months before both my father and my city fell. I felt confused. Peace reigns now, the peace we so longed for, so why am I depressed? I wondered.

My guard answered, as if he had been guarding my thoughts as well, "Ah, peace! How expansive peace is!"

I shifted my position, trying myself to expand a little in my seat, but the driver complained and I withdrew. Then he stopped the truck and asked me to move into its open back, saying, "Each of us sits in his own place."

There was no place for me to sit in the back, however, and so I remained standing. Soon we entered the Valley of Nasnas, moving up Jabal Street and passing the bakery belonging to the Armenian. I did not, of course, expect to see his little boy, whom I had taught Arabic, because the bakery door was barred.

"Get down!" my guard told me, and I did so. Then he handed me over to the Provisional Arab Committee.

They expressed their thanks at receiving me, but once the soldier had turned his back they swore at him. One of them exclaimed, "Do they think the premises of the committee is a hotel? We must protest this to the Office of the Minister for Minority Affairs!"

I wanted to assert my pride in being Arab, to impress them favorably, and expressed my distress at the change of the name of the city of Haifa to Medinah of Israel.

They gazed at one another in astonishment and one of them exclaimed, "And dim-witted, too!"

It took me a long time, right up to the first election campaign, to realize why they thought me dim witted. I then learned that the word *medinah* in Hebrew means "state." (Actually, they did preserve the name of Haifa because it occurs in the Bible.) By then, of course, I had quite convinced myself that I was in fact stupid. The best proof of this was that I had been the last of the committee members to realize that the late Kiork used to serve us donkey meat in his restaurant; and we used to eat it and thank him, mind you.

Next morning I went down to Kings' Street. There Adon Safsarsheck, in military uniform, received me at the entrance to his office. He gave me ten pounds and told me, "Your father served us. Take these and eat!" It was then that I began eating at Kiork's restaurant. One of the committee members found me an abandoned house belonging to an Arab of Haifa. After a while, however, some demobilized soldiers evicted me. And so I took employment as a leader in the Union of Palestine Workers.

Fourteen:

Saeed Takes Refuge in a Footnote

Footnote: Sometime recently, the world having in the meantime revolved completely on its axis, I read in your newspapers about an official request submitted by Hebron dignitaries to the military governor seeking permission to import asses from the East Bank. When asked where their asses had gone, the Hebron officials laughed and replied that Tel Aviv butchers had used them all to make sausages. You used to assure us, honored sir, that history, when repeating itself, does not reproduce itself precisely. If the first occurrence were tragedy, the second would be a farce.

So I ask you, which in this case is the tragedy and which the farce? Is there tragedy in the asses of the Valley of Nasnas, from so many destroyed villages, remaining free from chains and the burdens of women, with no one benefiting from their rich meat except the late Kiork? Or is there farce in all those delicious sausages being made in Tel Aviv?

I well know, my honored sir, how tenacious you are of the conclusions you deduce. But is it not true that whenever people leave their homes the asses remain, and whenever people stay the butchers find nothing to make into sausages except the meat of asses? Take this maxim from me: Many are the nations saved from a butcher's knife by an animal!

During my first days as a leader in the Union of Palestine

44

Workers, I entered many of the evacuated Arab homes in Haifa via their broken doors. I often found there cups still filled with coffee people had not had time to drink. So it was that I collected furniture for my home: some from this house, some from that. I was choosing from the leftovers that remained after my predecessors in the leadership had taken their share, having themselves been preceded by the Custodian of Abandoned Properties, who had taken his share. All of these had been preceded by Haifa's new elite, the one-time colleagues of Haifa's Arab elite. The last mentioned had left their villas, after assurances that the new elite would guard their property "just for a month or so," until their return. And so the new elite kept the property of the Arab elite in the "oriental salons" of their own villas in order to affirm an old and undying friendship as strong as oak. How they vaunted their "Abbas" carpets, named after the exclusive street in Haifa, just as their peers in Jerusalem took pride in their "Qatamun" carpets, named after the quarter in Jerusalem, which they had confiscated as well. The communists soon began to call the Custodian of Abandoned Properties the Custodian of Looted Properties. We cursed them, the Communists, in public but repeated what they said in private.

During the Six Day War, some years after the Tripartite Aggression in 1956,[25] which came after the War of Independence, I saw the people of Jerusalem, Hebron, Ramallah, and Nablus selling their wedding dishes for a pound apiece, and I thought, "One pound! My, that's cheap! Then I realized the truth of your deductions, that when history does repeat itself, honored sir, it brings a progression with it. For from *gratis*, we had moved to one pound. Things are truly progressing!

End of footnote.

Fifteen:

First Lesson in Hebrew

When I gained the position of leader in the Union of Palestine Workers, my courage placed me in a fix from which I could not have escaped had I not employed even greater courage.

Were it not for your friends, honored sir, who wrote about me and attacked me in their paper, so convincing me that I was important, the following events would never have occurred. Of course, worse things might have happened, I agree.

When I became certain I was important, I gathered my courage one afternoon and went by bus to the Valley of Camels, on the coast below Mt. Carmel lighthouse. There my father, God rest his soul, had built a house for us with the labor of that brother of mine who was torn to pieces by a crane. I told no one of my intention to undertake this adventure.

I crossed the railroad tracks, invoking God's mercy on our poet, Mutlaq Abdel Khaliq, run over by a train in 1937 as he was crossing the tracks at that very spot. Recalling the words of our great folk poet, Nuh Ibrahim, who said, "Religion is for God, but the country is for us all," I hurried over to Umm Asaad, who had spent her entire life since our childhood sweeping out the Catholic church there.

There I found her, sweeping the yard in exactly the same place we had left her. I said to myself, Praise be to God that nothing has changed, certainly not Umm Asaad's broom, made from thorn bush stalks.

I bent over to kiss her hand but she shouted angrily, "They've already had me, in the census." She then hurried inside to her room. I followed, not understanding what was wrong.

Umm Asaad walked straight to an icon of Our Lady Mary hung on the wall above her tidy bed and moved it aside to disclose a hole in the wall. From this she removed a package of white cloth which she unfolded, her back turned to me in order to conceal its contents. All the while she was repeating to herself, "O Virgin, this is the silver for my trousseau!"

Then she held out her hand with the neatly folded census papers and shouted with all the force her weak voice allowed, "I'm under the protection of our reverend bishop. What do you want with me, mister?"

"But Auntie, I'm Saeed," I protested. "How could you have forgotten me"?

"Saeed? Which Saeed?" she demanded.

"The one from al-Tira," I reassured her, knowing that in her valley they used to think that all country dwellers came from there. This made her positively dance with joy, and I gave her a big hug. Then we sat on the couch and she asked me about my mother and sister and about the yoghurt of al-Tira, indispensable for that famous delicacy Shaikh al-Mahshy.

"What about our house?" I asked at last.

"They are occupying it."

"Do you know who they are?"

"You can see, my child, how dim my eyes are. And Europeans all look the same, anyway. No one goes fishing anymore."

"Would they let me in if I visited our house?" I asked.

"How should I know, my son?"

She crossed herself. I said goodbye, feeling very uneasy that she had made that sign of the cross.

When I reached the front of our house and saw laundry hanging out, my courage deserted me and I pretended to be taking a stroll along the seashore. I kept passing back and forth in front of our house. Each time I almost knocked on the door my courage left me.

Eventually evening arrived. A woman emerged and began collecting the laundry. She stared at me and shouted something. I hurried away but saw a man of about her age come out of the house and help her collect the wash. I thought to myself: This must be a trick. Why else would a man bring in the family laundry? This was never done by my father, God have mercy on him, although my mother was always sickly and overworked.

I hurried away faster. Soon I came to the main road, which went past the villas that had belonged to the Arab officials of Haifa. They had built these before moving to Lebanon to build other villas only to leave them too. Darkness had now settled. I felt frightened and exhausted from this adventure, and I still had a long way to go.

Every now and then a Jewish worker would pass. I knew this from the work clothes they were wearing. They were middle-aged; all the young men and women were in the army. I needed to know the time in order to find out if a bus would come by or if they had stopped running for the day. In what language could I ask one of these people the time?

If I asked in Arabic they would discover my identity. If I asked in English they would grow suspicious. I was trying hard to remember the few words of Hebrew I knew when suddenly the right phrase came to me. It was, "Ma shaah?" This was a question I had once asked a girl near the Armon Cinema; she had responded by insulting my mother's honor in fine, high Arabic.

So I blurted out the same question to the next worker I saw. He hesitated, then smiled, looked at his wrist, and shouted, "Acht." I was no dummy and remembered that acht means "eight" in German. So I said a silent prayer for this neighbor of ours, a graduate of Schneller's School, and continued on foot toward the Valley of Nasnas, having made up my mind to learn Hebrew.

I remembered later what we had learned in school about how to decipher hieroglyphics. I began reading the names of shops in English, then comparing them with the Hebrew equivalent until I was able to recognize the letters. I followed this up by studying the Hebrew newspapers but began speaking the language before I had learned to read it. It was ten more years before I delivered my first

48

welcome address in Hebrew, which I did in the presence of Haifa's mayor, who registered it as a precedent.

But what is strange is that now, a quarter century later, the soapmakers of Nablus were able to learn Hebrew perfectly in less than two years. When one of them switched to the manufacture of marble tiles he hung up a sign in an easily read Kufic script of Arabic, saying that his premises made *shayesh*, followed by his own magnificently prolix and distinctively Arab name: *shayesh*, of course, is the Hebrew word for marble. This is not merely a case of necessity being the mother of invention; it is also a matter of the financial interests of a country's elite who cared so little who ruled them politically that they applied in practice the Arabic proverb: Anyone who marries my mother becomes my stepfather.

Sixteen:

Saeed Is No Longer an Ass

The day's events did not stop there. I was so impressed by the Jewish worker's ignorance of Hebrew that I decided that this state was not fated to survive. Why should I not therefore protect my line of retreat?

I told myself, Yes, the lawyer Isam al-Bathanjani—his name means the eggplant—the friend of my cousin the Jordanian minister, and dear to him as his own brother, is my last hope. He had converted his large house in Abbas Street into a kind of retreat from which he fulminated against the state of Adon Safsarsheck whenever a foreign journalist visited him. Even the Communists, whom the Minister of Minorities regarded as the most dangerous fifth column in the heart of the state, were viewed by this friend of my cousin the Jordanian minister as renegades and quite beyond the pale of Arabism and its religion.

He recognized neither the state nor its newspapers and adamantly refused to meet any but foreign journalists. His declarations therefore appeared only in the two Times, that of London and that of New York, as well as in the major newspapers in the Arab world. As for us, leaders in the Union of Palestine Workers, we whistled in amazement, our lips pursed, at his patriotic impudence when we heard he had refused to educate his son at the Hebrew University in Jerusalem. But when he sent him to Cambridge instead—Cambridge, no less!—we whistled in even greater astonishment.

When night came, I went to his home and knocked on the door. The smack of chips against a backgammon board ceased, and when the door was opened I saw him shaking the dice. I said, "Good evening." He was clearly surprised by my visit. A colleague of mine, a leader in the Union of Palestine Workers, had been playing there with him and was about to leave as I entered. I did not conceal my surprise at seeing him there. He greeted me, exclaiming, "He's my neighbor, you know!" I cleared my throat meaningfully and kept on doing so until he left.

I enumerated at length the known fine qualities of my cousin the Jordanian minister. When al-Bathanjani finally expressed his sorrow at my sad fate and his hope for my achieving forgiveness, I told him about my various adventures and how I felt about them all.

"May God ease it for you," he blessed me, but he provided no relief himself.

Next morning my feet had no sooner crossed the threshold of "the club" when my boss, Jacob called me to his office. Next to him, behind his desk, I saw a man of average height wearing dark glasses. The curtains of the room were all drawn. This man, I said to myself, must be blind.

I went up to him and shook his hand, not waiting for him to offer it to me, since I did not want to embarrass him over his blindness. But Jacob became furious and yelled, "Behave yourself!" I stood at attention.

"This is a very big man," Jacob explained. "He has come to speak to you in private; hide nothing from him."

Then he left us alone. As soon as the door closed behind Jacob the "big man" jumped to his feet, but his height scarcely increased by a hand's breadth.

"We know where you went yesterday," he yelled at me.

If this man is not blind, I said to myself, he certainly must be deaf! I went up to him and screamed in his ear, "I wanted a breath of sea air. Is that forbidden?"

He slapped me hard, his aim perfect. I said to myself, not deaf

51

nor blind, but definitely a big man. I therefore decreased my own size and replied, "Ask Adon Safsarsheck about me!"

"The old lady, Umm Asaad," he accused me.

"*Et tu,* Umm Asaad?" I said to myself.

"Acht!" he then screamed, his German pronunciation perfect.

And now he'll ask about that damned visit of mine to the Bathanjani house, I thought.

"And backgammon!" he shouted, confirming my worst fears.

I collapsed onto a chair, my head between my hands, shaking violently to and fro, just as my mother had taught us. Then I let out a moan. "By almighty God, I swear I know nothing about my cousin the Jordanian minister except his name!"

"Is he in fact your first cousin?" he demanded.

"No, by almighty God, no!" I insisted.

"Why not?" he enquired.

This question floored me. But he had calmed down and now he came closer to me and patted me on the shoulder in a fatherly manner: "Now let this be a lesson to you. You should realize that we have the latest equipment with which to monitor your every movement, even including what you whisper in your dreams. With our modern apparatus we know all that happens, both within the state and outside it. Take care you don't ever behave this way again."

I responded merely by continuing my violent shaking, repeating only, "I am an ass! I am an ass!"

I kept this up till he left, after he had finally removed his sunglasses. Then I began invoking God's mercy on my father's soul, for he had been the first person to discover what an ass I am.

But who cares anyway—God bless you, Umm Asaad, and you too, "Acht." By God Almighty I will go wherever I please, think whatever I want. But I was an ass, it's true, to knock on al-Bathanjani's door.

My father, God rest his soul, was right. He always used to beat me at backgammon and when I said to him, "You really are a champion at the game, father," he would reply, "No I'm not, my son. All my friends beat me. The fact is, you're just an ass!"

Determined to be an ass no more, I refrained from giving the big man my opinion of all his ultramodern equipment.

Seventeen:

Is Saeed the Hooded Informer?

My opinion about his equipment was fully formed now. If he had really been able to detect every single one of my movements he would definitely have marked down against me my strange meeting with the man from outer space. But this he had not done.

Feeling completely at ease on this score, I decided to revisit my extraterrestrial friend in the tunnels of Acre. He might need a word of warning, after all, and I certainly needed him.

I was therefore particularly subservient to my superiors all the next week, planning to slip over to Acre that Saturday, our day off.

The day I had chosen was the eleventh of December of that devil-cursed year, 1948. That unforgettable date marked both the end and the beginning of successive eras of my life.

That Friday evening I was holed up at home, trying to figure out the safest way to sneak into Acre the next morning. I had put out the light and gone to bed early to avoid a visit from my neighbor, an Armenian spinster. The fact is, I could only enjoy her company after we had got drunk. I thought of her then as my darling little Yuaad and she saw me as her great big Sarkis who had "run off with the Arabs," as she would say. She would enliven her intoxication by muttering in English about Clark Gable, Charles Boyer, and other stars. This affected me in a similar way, making me mutter things both repeatable and otherwise. The previous night I had kept cursing

53

Bathanjanis, that is eggplants, and all who favored them. This had made her put up a spirited defense of eggplants stuffed with meat and crushed wheat, and to shut me out. I had decided, therefore, that to be on the safe side I would not open the door for her that night.

So there I was, musing over matters such as these, when there was a knock on the door. Oh dear, I said to myself, she's come. But I won't open up nor apologize for my remarks about eggplants.

But the knocking persisted and temptation got the better of me. Maybe, I thought, I should open up but refrain from any mutterings at all. The knocking continued so I got up, telling myself that the electronic bug wouldn't understand Armenian anyway. And what were we, she and I, but two harmless, pitiable creatures. I opened the door.

There before me stood a woman of middle age, her cheeks somewhat pale, her eyes green. Her voice trembled as she asked shyly, "Saeed?"

I was speechless with surprise as I stared into those green eyes of hers and tried to remember where I'd seen that face. She had to be, I concluded, some relative from our village or perhaps from across the border. But whatever brought her here in the dead of night?

"Please come in," I whispered, uneasy though I felt.

"My sister Yuaad is downstairs. Can she come up?"

I could scarcely believe my eyes or ears. My habit, when I was overcome with longing for Yuaad, or had nothing else to do, was to sit or wander about, eyes open, but seeing only her. I would hold her hand, embrace her tightly, and we would sink together into joyful oblivion, never to return. On one occasion, in my office at the Union of Palestine Workers, I was actually knocked into a different unconsciousness by Aly Abu Mustafa, the cripple, who smacked me on the head with his cane because I had asked him to wait outside a few minutes but ended up by leaving him there for the best part of the day.

"Are you really Yuaad's sister?" I asked at last.

"Can she come up?"

"Yuaad! Yuaad!"

"Get back on up! You can't go down to her in your underclothes! Go inside and dress. I'll call her."

I took the advice of Yuaad's sister. I ran from room to room putting on clothes and tossing lipstick-stained cigarette butts into the toilet. Eventually, however, when I tried to flush it, it wouldn't draw. So I filled a pail with water and dumped it in, but the bowl overflowed onto the floor. I slipped and fell down on my hands and knees before the open door to find myself, in such a state, at the very feet of Yuaad, absent all those long years.

"Heaven reward you," she blessed me.

I rose to my feet, my face dripping both perspiration and toilet water. I collapsed into the nearest armchair and began to weep.

Yuaad and her sister rushed toward me, drying both water and tears, and did their best to assure me all could be made well.

But what did this imply? What was it that could be made well?

Yuaad chided me, "Now, Saeed. You know, God forgive you, what you did to my father and the rest."

But I, God forgive me, actually understood nothing.

The sister now told me that Yuaad had arrived on foot that day from Nazareth by way of the villages of Shafa Amr and Ibtin, alone over the mountains. She had come to tell her sister in Haifa that they had arrested their father in Nazareth and that I, Saeed, was the cause, since I had informed on him.

"Me?"

"Everyone says it was you," Yuaad insisted. "Are you really the hooded informer?"

"Me?"

"Like your father before you."

From all the charges and blaming that ensued, mixed with tears and solemn protestations sworn by me that I was quite incapable of wanting to harm anyone at all, especially not Yuaad's family, I learned that her father had moved their home from Haifa to Nazareth after the Haifa refinery was blown up the first time. When the capital of Galilee—Nazareth, that is—fell, the Israeli army demanded that everyone give up their weapons. When the mayor told them there were no weapons except for backgammon boards around which all the men gathered the instant the curfew was lifted, they began put-

55

ting concerted pressure on the city. First they cordoned off the eastern quarter, where Yuaad's family had taken refuge. Then they crammed all the men into a vacant lot near the well behind the Coptic church, keeping them there all day in the burning heat without water. And this despite the fact that a well brimmed right there beneath their feet with holy water from the sacred Virgin's Spring.

Yuaad related proudly how she had reminded the Communists of that ancient verse which they subsequently used as the title of the pamphlet they distributed during the siege:

> *Like desert camels of thirst dying*
> *While on their backs water bearing.*

The military governor assembled them all. He denied that his army had prevented the camels and other such animals from drinking water from the well during the operation. The men did their best to explain that the verse was only allegorical. This made him extremely angry and he defended with spirit the dignity of man, insisting that he should never be compared with a beast of burden, not even if an Arab, an enemy. He said, "You have become citizens, precisely like us." He then had them herded out of his sight.

During the cordon operation the army took aside all those the hooded informer singled out and transferred them to the prison camps as prisoners of war. Yuaad's father had been among them.

"What is this hooded informer business?" I asked.

"He is a man," Yuaad explained, "whose head is covered with a sack with three holes in it, two for his eyes and one for his mouth. They have him sit at a table surrounded by soldiers. As our men pass in front of the table the soldiers scrutinize them, and if the sack nods twice the man indicated is led away from the rest. They took, in a single operation, at least five hundred men and boys as prisoners of war.

"Why did you do it, Saeed?"

56

Eighteen:

Saeed's First Night Alone with Yuaad

At last I did convince Yuaad and her sister that I was not the hooded informer. But as it turned out I became, after that night, as worthless as an old sack.

Yuaad had come from Nazareth to Haifa without permission from the authorities and was therefore an infiltrator. The authorities used to force their way into houses at all hours of the day and night searching out infiltrators, and if they found any they would remove them under cover of darkness to the outskirts of Jinin, to the plain situated between that town and the village of Muqaiblah, where the British army used to have a base.

When the British had evacuated that base they had left behind many buried land mines, to which the Arab and Jewish soldiers had added more, because the first line of conflict was there. After the war finally ground to a halt, one of the mines exploded under some boys from the village of Sandala who stepped on it when returning home from school. Seventeen were killed, according to the official statement, not counting those wounded who were to die later.

Immediately after this incident, Jacob, my boss, summoned us all and delivered a lecture against the Communist—anti-Semites, as he said—who instigate people to strike and demonstrate and who were claiming that it had been an Israeli mine. He went on to state, moreover, that our committee, the Union of Palestine Workers, was

57

a democratic organization in a democratic state and that therefore we were free to announce that the mine had been left either by the British or by the Arabs.

When our left-handed colleague al-Shalfawi (his right hand was paralyzed) mentioned that the Communist statement included an accusation that the government had neglected to clear the road of mines from the war, Jacob replied, "We are well aware that your brother-in-law is one of them!" Thereafter al-Shalfawi's tongue was paralyzed as well.

To get back to where we were, we finally agreed that it would not be safe for the "infiltrator" Yuaad to stay at her sister's home. The latter and her children had not evacuated their house in al-Halisah: she was awaiting the return of her husband, who had gone out one morning saying he'd be back soon.

As we were agreeing that Yuaad would stay that night in a separate room in my house, I kept my eyes to the floor. I was apprehensive that they might hear how my heart was pounding.

Yuaad's sister pleaded with me on my sister's honor to protect her sister's honor, adding, "You can have her later, if you like, legally!"

Finally she said goodbye and left. I was by now feeling quite overcome by all this. In my mind the long-lost honor of my sister had become intertwined with Yuaad, whom I had met again so suddenly. She went to her room, locked the door, and began weeping and sobbing loudly, while I lay there stretched out on my bed before her door, able neither to sleep nor to get up. Thus we remained, she sobbing incessantly and me still lying there.

Suddenly I heard her call out, "Saeed!" I pretended to be asleep. "Saeed!" I held my breath.

At last she opened the door. I shut my eyes tight. I felt her arranging the bed cover over me and then heard her footsteps move slowly to the bathroom. I listened as she took a bath and went back to her room, now leaving the door between us open slightly.

How could I get up now? She would know I had been awake throughout and would wonder why I had not responded to her call. She had been my first love and from that night on she would be my eternal love. How, then, could I have her sleep in the same house with me and not even say a single word to her? Or exchange a single kiss? Was I just too scared? Why wasn't I scared with Sarkis's girlfriend then?

What was I to do? How long should I stay lying there on the bed?

Not for long, as it turned out.

Nineteen:

"Don't Worry, Saeed! I'll Return to You!"

Well, there I lay, holding my breath like a child who has wet his bed awaits some miracle to save him from the catastrophe of discovery, with the dawn, that eternal infiltrator, coming at me from the east through the window. Suddenly there was a violent knocking at the door. This sent me right into Yuaad's room, shaking in terror. She was standing there completely dressed.

"Have they come?" she asked.

"I don't know," I replied.

"Who is that knocking?"

"I have no idea."

"Shut me in and don't tell them I'm here! On your honor, now."

The knocking grew louder and we heard loud voices.

"Oh my love, my life." I whispered.

"Not now! Not now!"

"You are mine!"

"Later, later!"

"No! Now, now!"

She pulled away from me, took my hand, and fled into my room. We fell down together onto the bed. At that moment we heard the door break open, and my left rib felt as if it were breaking, too.

I closed the door on her and stood ready to confront them in my pajamas.

It was soldiers.

"Search!"

"Why did you break down the door?"

A soldier pushed me aside, and they spread out into the house, searching cupboards and ransacking drawers.

"Are you alone here!"

"Alone."

I put on my shirt and trousers and placed myself before the door of the room where Yuaad was hiding. I took out an identity card showing that I belonged to the Union of Palestine Workers and referred them to Adon Safsarsheck. They stopped searching.

However, the soldier who seemed in charge was suspicious about the room behind the closed door. He tried to push me away and open it, but I refused to budge.

"Open it!" he shouted.

"There's nothing there," I insisted.

His temper flared and he made straight for the door. I stretched my arms out full length, determined to die a martyr. He looked over to his men and laughed, but they did not. He ordered them to seize me, but they hesitated. Then he screamed an order at them, and this time they came at me together, overcame me, threw me outside, then hurled me down the stairs from the third floor. Hands kept receiving me and then tossing me further down until I reached the bottom. There I found myself at Jacob's feet, still clutching my Union of Palestine Workers identity card, trying but failing to hold it up high enough for him to read.

"I know who you are, you ass!" he yelled. "Get up and tell me what's going on."

But I did not. For at that moment we heard a woman's screams coming from above, along with the noise of slapping and kicking, an enormous din. We stared up and saw a furious battle raging between Yuaad and the soldiers who were hurling her down the stairs. Other soldiers stood around pretending not to see what was happening. She kept resisting, shouting, and kicking. When Yuaad bit one soldier on the shoulder, he screamed in pain and retreated.

Their pushing and her resistance and kicking went on until they finally managed to throw her out onto the stairway. She landed on her own two feet, her body straight and her head held high.

"She's an infiltrator!" a soldier explained, panting.

"This is my country, this is my house, and this is my husband!" she retorted loudly.

Jacob swore a four-letter curse. She promptly referred the word to his own mother. They crowded about her and shoved her into a car full of others like herself. Then the car drove off.

As the car moved I could hear her yelling to me at the top of her voice, "Saeed! Don't worry, Saeed! I'll return to you!"

Meanwhile, I still lay there, stretched out on the pavement.

Twenty:

The Open Wound

Years and years I had spent waiting for her to come back.

They had taken her with other "infiltrators" to Haifa: people from Nazareth, Jaffa, Maalul, Shafa Amr, Iblin, and Tamrah. Many an Arab worker who had slipped into the city to feed his family had also been seized. They left them on the Jinin plain, amidst the land mines of the British, the Arabs, and the Jews.

Some of them hid in the ruins, others amongst the trees, and did not cross over into Jordan. They moved while it was dark and slept by day, returning whence they had come, only to be expelled again, to return, to be expelled, and then to return once more, right up to the present time.

Some of them did keep on walking until Jordanian soldiers met them with curses, and they are still swearing at them today.

Yuaad was among those who did not return. A returning "infiltrator" one day secretly put in my hand a piece of paper. It was a letter from her. I refrained from reading it until I was certain that there were no electronic bugs about. This is the only confidential paper I have kept all this time to convince myself that I was capable of defying the "equipment" and because I regard it as a marriage certificate.

Yuaad wrote:

I beg anyone who finds this letter to take it to my husband, Saeed Pessoptimist, the Ill-fated, in Haifa.

Saeed! Saeed! My husband! Farewell, farewell, my love! I await death at the borders but shall die certain that you will save my father from prison. Greet my sister and take care of her children. Farewell, farewell, my love!

Your wife,
Yuaad.

I learned, however, that she did not die, and so I considered myself to have a wife in Jinin or in one of the refugee camps. I began to take an interest in the official "family reunification" program. I was also careful to listen in often to the messages broadcast on Amman radio by expatriates to their families. I never did dare to send her my greeting on the "Greet Your Loved Ones" program on Israeli radio. That show always began with a sadly sentimental song by the famous singer Farid al-Atrash: "Our loved ones, my heart, are not with us./ We went and they left us,/ None of them waited for us, my heart, Oh heart of mine." I used to wipe the tears from my eyes surreptitiously so that the bug would not see me cry. Eventually every Arab radio station broadcast such programs, each beginning with a song like, "We shall return," or "Greetings, people of the occupied land./ You remaining firm there in your homes,/ my heart is with you." Or "Oh messenger in chief on the nearby road,/ Take this handkerchief from me as you go on your way,/ And give it to my love." Ultimately all these songs seemed to merge into a strange medley, and I lost Yuaad completely.

When the Six Day War broke out and the ominous voice of the "messenger in chief" began to intone, "A victory from God and an imminent conquest," I ceased crying for Yuaad and began doing so for myself—and regardless of concern for bugs.

But to return to earlier days; Jacob did take pity on me. He followed us to the square where they had crammed us in the corner between Jabal Street and Abbas Street and extracted me before the sorting began and before I encountered the hooded informer. When I told him what had happened to Yuaad, he critized me for not telling the soldiers the truth from the very first moment. But he did promise to arrange with the authorities to have Yuaad found—"even if she is in Qatar!"—and returned to me.

"But on one condition, Saeed: that you be a good boy."

"Yes, sir!"

"And serve us faithfully."

"Yes, sir!"

And all that was to protect the future of poor Yuaad, whom he promised to return to me.

"Of course," he added, "the matter will take some time."

But the matter took forever. Before each election he would convince me that immediately after the votes were counted he would take me to the Mandelbaum Gate in Jerusalem to receive Yuaad. "So show us what you can do!" he would say.

I therefore never rested, never slept, in order to continue my pursuit of the Communists. I plotted against them, organized attacks on them, and gave witness against them. I would infiltrate demonstrations, tip over garbage cans in their way, and yell slogans advocating the destruction of the state to provide the police an excuse to attack them. I would whisper into the ears of conservative old men that the Communists tore up the Koran, and I would sit on ballot boxes from six o'clock in the morning till midnight. But the only reward I got for all this was the repeated promise of Yuaad's return.

Meanwhile, all my colleagues doing similar things were getting promoted to those positions reserved for Arabs; al-Shalfawi became a member of the Knesset, and Nazmi al-Shawish[27] became a sergeant; Abd al-Fattah Dahin Zuqmah became a school principal, his wife a school principal, and his daughter a teacher, but his son fell into the hands of the Communists and they sent him to study medicine in Moscow.

No one remained unrewarded except Jacob and me. I became his reward. When they amalgamated the Union of Palestine Workers with the Histadrut, they appointed him an official in the Department of Arab Affairs, with me under him.

The great energy I always showed in his service did not, however, save me from Jacob's anger; nor did it save him from the fury of that big man of small stature who wore dark glasses in rooms with drawn curtains. As soon as the election results appeared Jacob would rant and rave and shout, "There will be no Yuaad for you! How did you allow the Communists to win so many votes?"

"Me?"

"All right, forget it. Let's try once again."

But despite all my deeds, I kept a clear conscience: I wanted to meet Yuaad again. Finally I got married, and then the secret agreement between Jacob and myself to bring back Yuaad began to haunt me, as though it were a betrayal of my marriage.

And on this wound Jacob began to press with all his might.

BOOK TWO: BAQIYYA[28]—THE GIRL WHO STAYED

As a mother loves
Her mutilated child
I love this,
My beloved country.

Salim Joubran

Twenty–one:

Saeed Reports That "Reasons of Security" Made Him Stop Writing

Saeed Pessoptimist, the ill-fated, wrote to me later and addressed me as follows:

Greetings! And the mercy and blessings of God be upon you! I haven't written for some time for reasons of security—this time mine and not the state's, as well as that of my brothers from outer space, with whom I now live in the catacombs of Acre, safe but not secure.

When the government began renovating the catacombs, re-building their walls, putting in electric lighting, clearing the halls and the decorative work and restoring them, we began retreating into other invisible tunnels. Now we never remain in one place, never can feel at ease with ourselves, not for a single moment. It is all rather like those expressions of yours, you know, "hit and run," "eat on the run," "write on the run." But this is not, in fact, possible.

When summer was over the trespassers became rare. The din subsided, and the only noise was from a frog praying or a cockroach taking communion.

My companion from outer space summoned me and said, "Let's go out to the sea." So we went and sat down on an enormous, smooth rock set in a hollow in the wall to the left of the lighthouse. We threw out our lines hoping to find fish.

It was October. The breeze came warmly from the east, and the sea was calm, its quiet surface reflecting a scattering of stars. We gazed before us and saw that Haifa, lit up in brilliance, had become two. One city reclined on the pillow of Mount Carmel, while the other swam there in the sea, stripped of its earrings, rings, and necklaces.

As I gazed out at the mighty sea, so calm before us, it struck me how powerful it looked. True power is expressed in quiet confidence; it was the sea's very calmness that epitomized its mighty force.

How very many a disturbed soul, like mine, had sought refuge in the sea and had found comfort in its quiet confidence.

During those terrible nights of the June War, Arab men flocked there to fish. They were avoiding, it was said, the nagging of their wives. But in reality they were searching in the sea for reassurance that there was something stronger than our state.

Many a night as they stood there on the rocks of Nahariyah, where the sea swallows the town's sewage to fertilize the fish, the police would make a sudden appearance. The calm security of the sea made the fishermen feel bold. Taking the questions from the police too lightly, they would end up spending the rest of the night in jail.

It was this pastime, fishing, that gave me a very strange secret, the preservation of which became my lifelong occupation. Had I not taken refuge with my extraterrestrial brothers in the catacombs of Acre, where your evil cannot reach me, I would have carried this secret with me to the grave.

Recalling this secret of mine, I observed to my companion, "Such strange mysteries there are in these parts!"

My friend from outerspace responded with the comment, "Ibn Jubair,[29] the traveler who visited Acre in 1158, preceded you in this conclusion. He sat on this very shore waiting for the sea to calm so that he could flee from this city that had been adulterated by the Byzantines. He later wrote, 'There is a strange mystery in the way the wind blows in these parts. For it comes from the east only in the spring and autumn and so only then can people travel. Merchants land their goods at Acre only in these two seasons. The springtime travel season is from the middle of April until the end of May or thereabouts, as God wills. Voyages recommence in autumn, in the middle of October. But the autumn season is shorter—in fact, only around fifteen days, give or take a little. At other times of year the winds are mixed; the west wind being the most predominant. Travelers to North Africa, Sicily, and Greece await the east wind with all the expectancy of a promise to be fulfilled. Blessed be God in all his wisdom, his power invincible, the one and only God.' "

And I joined in this praise. I recalled how, during this very short period each year, the Arab fishermen of Acre would sail far out to sea in their tiny boats to net the enormous *bellamidas* which they could hardly drag aboard. That's a "foreign" fish, one that Arab women don't know how to cook very well.

My companion also observed: "This sea calms down each spring and autumn, the best seasons in this lovely country of yours. It is then that all those people arrive who so fall in love with it that they stay, settling in wave after wave, layer above layer. That's why archaeology is the only science suitable for the study of the ruins and the history of this area."

And I replied: "Yes, it was in the spring that I met the woman from Tantura, and in the fall that I lost her son. How brief a time elapsed, it seems, between those two seasons."

Twenty-two:

The Amazing Similarity between Candide and Saeed

My extraterrestrial friend was quite startled whenever a jet roared past, coming and going over the sea, flying north to Ras al-Naqurah and beyond, finally disappearing over the mountains. Each time he jumped, I thought a frightened fish had pulled on his line, and I tugged lightly on mine and then relaxed again.

Once he commented, "I've been thinking about the reactions of the 'friends' of your friend to what he published of that first letter you sent him. They said he had' . . . taken steps toward a great leap forward but had ended up falling short of Candide by a couple of hundred years.' "

"But what does it have to do with him?" I objected. "My friend is only a messenger boy. And the function of a messenger is merely to pass on the message."

My companion also complained that "Candide was an optimist, but you're a pessoptimist."

"That fact," I responded, "is a virtue that, above all others distinguishes my people."

"But you," he criticized again, "seem to be imitating Candide."

"Don't blame me for that. Blame our way of life that hasn't changed since Voltaire's day, except that El Dorado has now come to exist on this planet."

"Do you mind explaining that?"

And explain indeed I did, by establishing a full and accurate analogy between us and Candide, leaving out only those repetitive circumstances that had occurred year in and year out over the past quarter-century. Finally I observed: "Did not Pangloss express consolation for the Abarian women who had been raped, and who had seen bellies ripped open, heads cut off, and their castles demolished, with the comment: 'But we've had our revenge, for the Abares have done the very same thing to a neighboring barony, which belonged to a Bulgarian lord.'?

"We ourselves, after all, sought consolation in the same way two hundred years later. That was in September 1972, when our athletes were killed in Munich. Did our military aircraft not 'take revenge' for us by murdering women and also children, just beginning to enjoy the 'sport' of life, in refugee camps in Syria and Lebanon? Didn't this 'console' us? In October of that same year, our planes having returned after bombing Syrian refugee camps, did not our very own Pangloss, the Minister of Education and Culture Yigael Allon, meet with the widows of our athletes who had fallen victim and console them by saying that our aircraft had hit all their targets and had done a magnificent job?

"And even years before, in early July 1950, when our state was still learning to crawl and, gazing out at the world with all the innocence of babyhood, did not our much-famed author Jon Kimche express the same Pangloss-like wisdom when he wrote in the *Jerusalem Post*: 'The Arabs waged a bloody war against the Jews. And they were defeated. So they have no right to complain when they are asked to pay the price for the defeat which they have suffered.'!

"Then there's Candide himself, who 'resolved one fine day in spring to go for a walk, marching straight before him, believing that it was a privilege of the human as well as of the animal species to make use of their legs as they pleased. He had advanced two leagues when he was overtaken by four others, heroes six foot tall, who bound him and carried him to a dungeon.'

"Compare that with the case of some children of the village of al-Tiba, ranging in age from nine to twelve years old, who used that same human and animal privilege and went for a walk to the town of Natanya to see the ocean, the surge of whose waves they had up to then only heard. They too were arrested. Brought before a military court, they were sentenced by the judge to pay a fine. If they lacked the resources for the fine, they had to pay with what they did have—namely, their lives, to the extent of one month in prison. When one of the children was unable to pay the fine, his father offered to stay one month in jail. But this the judge refused, insisting instead that the boy's mother add one month to the nature-prescribed nine of pregnancy by spending one in jail for him. This verdict was issued in May 1952.

"This same 'human privilege' is still, right up to the present day, entirely dependent on the permission of a governor.

"And you remember in *Candide*, when the corsairs seized their ship on the high seas and began searching the men and women, how the old servant woman related, 'It's amazing with what speed those gentlemen undress people. But what surprised me most was that they thrust their fingers into the part of our bodies which most women allow no instrument other than a medical syringe to enter. It appeared to me a very strange kind of ceremony; but thus one judges of things when one has not seen the world. I afterwards learned that it was to discover whether we had concealed any diamonds. This is an established practice since time immemorial among civilized nations that scour the seas. I was informed that the very religious Knights of Malta never fail to make this search when they take Turkish prisoners of either sex. It is a law of nations from which they never deviate.'

"Why, our government still applies this same 'international law' to Arab prisoners of either sex, on land, on sea, and in the air, in the airport at Lydda, at the port of Haifa, and over the 'open bridges.' That's why our 'Turks of either sex,' when they decide to travel, take such pains to clean out their pockets, suitcases, and clothes, inside and out. And our 'Turkish' ladies are careful to wear the very finest nylon underwear, to inspire awe and envy in the policewomen who search them and so ensure that they behave themselves."

My outer-space friend laughed at that and asked humorously, "Do you really think your friend's 'friends' complaint that he pla-

74

giarized *Candide* results from the fact that when they strip people naked they put their fingers in there?"

"Anyway," I said, "there's no real comparison at all. Pangloss, after all, consoled his womenfolk who had had their bellies ripped open by telling them that their own soldiers had done the same to the women of their enemy. But the Arabs of Israel are victims of both armies, the Abares and the Bulgarians."

"Give me an example."

"Well, take the village of Bartaa, in the 'triangle', divided, like the child at the court of Solomon, peace be upon him, into two halves, one Jordanian and the other Israeli."

"Yes, but that child at the court of King Solomon, peace be upon him, remained in one piece. His real mother refused to have him divided up."

"In Bartaa's case they did divide it, but it nevertheless remained whole. Once some thieves rustled a herd of ten cattle, and the Jordanians found that the tracks led to Bartaa. They sent a troop of cavalry to assault the village. It was on November 21, 1950, that the attack came. The soldiers knocked the villagers to the ground and beat and kicked them till they had had their fill. And then the villagers got up and fed the soldiers till they had had their fill, providing a couple of chickens for each, as well as fodder for the horses. They all had a fine time. But when they left, in came Pangloss's troops, spreading throughout the village, seeking anyone who had collaborated with the Jordanian raiders.

"Any villager they discovered who had not actually been thrown to the ground but who had been only beaten they considered guilty of having collaborated. And anyone thrown to the ground but only kicked was also seen as a collaborator. And so on and so forth.

"So I'd like to bring this strange comparison between us and *Candide* to an end with one statement: namely, Candide, my dear sir, used to say, 'All is well with the world.' One must admit, however, that one might well groan a little at what goes on in this world of ours, both mentally and physically. But in my case, it wasn't possible for me to so much as raise a groan."

"Can you explain that?" asked my outer-space friend.

"I will indeed explain."

Twenty-three:

Saeed Changes into a Cat That Meows

I lived in the outside world—outside the tunnels, that is—for twenty years, unable to breath no matter how I tried, like a man who is drowning. But I did not die. I wanted to get free but could not; I was a prisoner unable to escape. But I did remain unchained.

How often I yelled at those about me, "Please, everyone! I groan at the burden of the great secret I bear on my shoulders! Please help me!" But all that came from beneath my moustache was a meowing sound, like that of a cat.

Eventually I came to believe in the transmigration of souls.

Imagine your soul, after your death, entering a cat and this cat being resurrected and roaming around your house. Then imagine your son, whom you love so dearly, going out to play as all children do, and you calling him, meowing to him again and again, while he tells you again and again to shut up. Finally he throws a stone at you. This makes you retreat, reciting to yourself the words of our great poet al-Mutanabbi[30] in the gardens of Buwan in Persia: "In face, hand, and tongue a stranger."

That's how I've been for twenty years, meowing and whimpering so much that this idea of transmigration has become a reality in my mind. Whenever I see a cat, I feel uneasy, thinking that this might be my mother, may her soul rest in peace. So I smile at it, pet it, and even exchange meows with it.

This made my outer-space friend smile, and he commented, "Do take it easy, old son of Ill-fated. I see you're ready to graduate to initiation into the high ninth stage of the philosophic system of the mystical Ismaili[31] sect!

"Our forebears," he continued, "in the secret group of loyal friends known as the Brethren of Purity, the *Ikhwān al-Safā*,[32] used to consider people like you to be like beasts of burden, tied together with heavy iron bridles and halters so that they could be led anywhere and could be kept from saying what they might want to say. Thus they would remain until God allowed them to emerge from their stupor, to rise up and resist. This would occur following the appearance of the Voice of God personified. He would set free these people chained like beasts of burden, these people living in the degradation of captivity, humiliated and enslaved by those ruling them. He would then punish those who had abused them by placing them in chains in their stead."

"Give me that voice!" I exclaimed.

"Continue writing to your friend."

"But he introduces me to the people as though I'm different from them."

"But how are you different from one of their poets? You happen to be changed into a cat, they into poets. You each take flight to breathe and suppress your words in order not to perish. Many adopt literature becasue they lack power for anything more, while others avoid taking a stand by moving abroad.

"Others clothe the shame of their impotence with a paper wisdom, others with 'philosophy,' certain that the clock of time will transport them slowly on its small hand, even if not quickly on its large, right on up to the hour of judgment. They pretend that 'the people' are incapable of anything more and adopt other such excuses of the weak.

"But a thousand years ago our leader Abu Rukwah[31] did not do so. When he saw that his sultan, who bore the title Governor by Right of God, was ruling with tyranny, he did not feel helpless, and wait for the people to become fit to fight. He adopted the title Rebel by Right of God and conquered power with power. Since the ruler was more at fault, many people followed the rebel, ourselves among them."

"But what about the secret I bear?" I asked.

"Tell it to the world," he advised.

And that is what I am doing.

Twenty-four:

Saeed Anticipates Real Arab Nationalism by a Frenzy of Work in a Frenetic Age

One spring I met a girl from Tanturah,[34]—Tanturiyya let's call her. This is not her real name, of course, but a reference to her village lying beside the sea. There she was born thirteen years before that village fell. The eviction of the villagers came suddenly, while she was visiting relatives in the hamlet of Jisr al-Zarqa, which also lies on the coast. She remained there, perhaps fated to share my troubles with me if only for a season.

The story of this hamlet, Jisr al-Zarqa, is a strange one. How was this tiny place along with its sister village, Fraydis—"Paradise," that is—able to withstand the catastrophes of war and dispossession, when such gales tore up all the other Arab villages on the shore between Haifa and Tel Aviv? The list[35] is long—al-Tirah, 'Ain Hawd, al-Mazar, Jaba', Ijzim, Sarafand, Kufr Lam, 'Ain Ghazal, al-Tanturah, al-Buraikah, Khirbat al-Burj, Qaisariyyah, Umm Khalid, Khirbat al-Zababidah, al-Haram, Jalil al-Shamaliyyah, and Jalil al-Qibliyyah. Weren't these in fact stronger and more deeply rooted than Fraydis? Yet it survived to fulfil a purpose that Jacob had in mind.

Now this Jacob was not my master Jacob of the Union of Palestine Workers but a certain James (Jacob) de Rothschild who had established nearby the colony of Zikhron Yaqub "in memory of

Jacob," at the close of the nineteenth century. Its settlers, who had all come from Europe, began producing fine wines. Nowadays the summer resorts of the Arab world place these wines, which have acquired so many different names, on the tables of Arabian princes from the Empty Quarter. The wines reach them via the "open bridges" across the Jordan, and the princes enjoy them mightily. Their songsters celebrate it thus, in the very poetry of the ancients:

> *Oh Bishr, no swords, no wars for me;*
> *My star for fun and frolic stands,*
> *Song, wine, lovely dancers to see,*
> *And sleep with a sweet girl demands;*
> *Now there's an Arab Knight to be!*

Then these drunken princes roar in fury, accusing of treason those who demand implementation of the resolutions of the United Nations Security Council!

Yes, it's a fact that the people of Fraydis were saved from the storms of war by the grape juice in Yaqub's jars. It's true to say that they make huge profits at Zikhron Yaqub, won from the toil and sweat of the people of Fraydis.

These settlers, then, laughed good-naturedly when the following story about them spread (it was related to me by my master Jacob). The elders of Zikhron Yaqub disagreed about the following problem: Is it lawful for a man to sleep with his wife on the sabbath, or is the act a kind of work and therefore not lawful on that day? They went to the rabbi for a decision as to whether it was work or pleasure. The rabbi thought long and hard, and then he ruled that it was pleasure. They asked him for his reasoning. He replied: "If I had ruled it to be work, you would have given it to the Arabs of Fraydis to perform!"

My, how we laughed at this story—Jacob because he hates the Ashkhenazi or "Western" Jews, and I because he laughed.

And who would be so unfair as to blame the people of Fraydis for owing their preservation to vintage wine? Who, after all, erected the tall buildings of this country, cut and paved its broad streets, dug the trenches, and fortified the shelters? Who planted, plucked, and ginned the cotton, then wove it into clothes for the lords of Raghdan and Basman, palaces in Amman, to wear so proudly? It was said that the National Union would have them make one standardized uniform from this cloth, so that all its members would be equal to one another, similar as the teeth on a comb. And then no Arab would feel himself better than any non-Arab, except for their kings and for the way they wear their *kuffiyya*, their headdress, the very symbol of their national identity. When their Arab blood boils they muffle their faces in the *kuffiyyas* and silently invoke the name of God. When it bursts within them they squat down, fuming and foaming about a "better life" and hold forth against all "foreign imports." Except, that is, for kingship, cloth for *kuffiyyas*, air planes, bars, photographs (both to take and to pose for), the kissing of hands, the crown prince, and "how the rich enjoy the hunger of the poor," to quote Ali[36] the son of Abu Talib. And that's not to mention exploitation and injustice to workers, with livelihoods being cut off, and debauchery in this age of skirts raised high. Yes, who erected the buildings, paved the roads, dug and planted the earth of Israel, other than the Arabs who remained there? Yet those Arabs who stayed, stoically, in land occupied by our state received never so much as a mention in all the files of Ahmad Shukairy's[37] ringing speeches.

How often in Ajami Square in Jaffa I have seen those fresh-faced young men from Gaza, Jabaliyya and so on, swaying in the back of contractors' trucks, like the tombstones of those martyred brothers that have been seen moving in a Gaza graveyard. I have come to believe that the living too can indeed remain in their own land.

When I see such men in Lower Haifa, there in Paris Square, (previously known as Hanatir ("carriage") Square and before that as Khamrah Square), awaiting the trucks of the contractors, who will feel their arms and scrutinize their trim bodies and then pick out those with the strongest arms and the firmest legs, I recall how we were twenty years ago and have faith that this nation of ours will never die. At sunset I often see them again being crammed into old trucks just as they have all day crammed boxes of potatoes and piles of beetroots into trucks newer than the ones that will transport them

81

back to their towns and villages at night. Except, that is, for those whom Mr. Contractor pretended not to see and allowed to spend the night in some unfinished building. These workers must cover themselves with bricks to protect themselves from their two likely attackers, the early morning cold and the nighttime police. When dawn arrives, they will roll up their sleeves and start working again.

Seeing them reminds me how we were twenty years ago, and how my master Jacob would ask me to choose between losing Tanturiyya, as I had lost Yuaad before, or rising at dawn to visit the workers who had fallen into the clutches of contractors, to save them from the claws of the Communists, "just as the old Christian women saved the priest's beard from being plucked as he stood in prayer before the altar."★

I came to believe that all this was our predetermined fate, and that "what will be will be," as in the Italian song, the sense of which may be translated poetically thus:

> *The path we're fated for, that we walk;*
> *All fated with a path, that we stalk.*

But the people of the village of Jisr al-Zarqa, close relatives of my Tanturiyya, did not walk a single step. They never left their undiscovered village: that is the secret of their survival. They remained, fishing at the river's mouth, safe and secure.

All except her, that is, my Tanturiyya.

★This is in reference to the ostracism of the communists by the Vatican at the beginning of the fifties. A rumor circulated in Haifa to the effect that the communists had planned to pluck the beard of the priest, and that that was the reason for their ostracism by the Church.

Twenty-five:

Saeed Relates How Crocodiles Once Lived in the River Zarqa

In the early fifties I often went fishing off the steep rocks where the sea is deep at the mouth of the river Zarqa, where crocodiles once lived. Our brethren the Jews later gave it their own name, Dragon River, though nothing lives in it now but those little fish called mullet, along with a few eels. There at the river mouth, before the sun sank into the sea, I would see the boys and girls, their slim bodies bronze and ebony black, plunge naked into the water. Positioning themselves in parallel lines in the river, they would advance together toward the sea. They would hold their hands down in the water and would bring them out at intervals gripping wriggling fish. These they would throw onto the beach. The women there would gather them and put them into sacks.

My girl, my Tanturiyya, blonde like a Byzantine, would not participate in this, but would always stand a little off. Her eyes alone took part in this strange fishing scene; they shone with vitality. Her lips moved occasionally too, recording in quick and uneasy smiles the wriggling of the fish being thrown onto the beach.

She was the same age as the other boys and girls, around fourteen or fifteen, as fresh as the dawn itself in these parts of the country, but she was different from them in the very way she stood apart and in the ivory lightness of her complexion.

Since I knew that the other children were descendants of men who had been brought to Palestine by Ibrahim Pasha from eastern Egypt, and who had settled in Jisr al-Zarqa and other villages on this shore, I concluded that this lone blondè girl might be descended from some Greek slave and might thus be a relative of ours. So I began observing her very closely for a variety of reasons, some historical, others not.

When she noticed my presence and lowered her eyes in modesty, and I saw the blush of the rosy twilight reflected in her fresh young face, and then when she raised her eyes and I saw in them surprise and uncertainty and a vivaciousness that made me think of the *dabka* as it is danced in the north, I knew I was done for.

How I yearn for those days! For now not only the village of Tanturah but also its girl are gone. And the people of Jisr al-Zarqa have changed as well. They put their clothes back on, left the sea, and joined their neighbors who work the land, the people of Fraydis. Now none of them go down to the river or stand where it joins the sea, except for children playing truant and old men trying to escape the burdens of their age. And had it not been for the Nature Conservation Committee and the laudable campaign it conducted which succeeded in preventing the authorities from building an electric power station at the mouth of the river, my name, Saeed, would not remain carved on that limestone rock where Tanturiyya used to rest while we wove with our glances the fabric of our future.

Twenty-six:

Baqiyya, the Girl Who Would Share Her Secret with Saeed Before She Would Her Life

As I walked along the shore one evening, with no one else about, I happened to lean on that rock and saw my name carved there on its top. I realized that the young Tanturiyya was braver than the young man I was. She must have questioned the children to whom I gave fishing hooks to buy off their mischief, and thus discovered my name.

So I knew then that she loved me; and I therefore loved her. I have always known that I will inevitably fall in love with any woman who loves me. I just wish now that I had realized then that her courage was indeed most extraordinary. But in fact I was already drowned in love as I leaned there on top of that limestone rock.

I made a point of giving lots of hooks and nylon lines to one boy I knew who would go down into the sea for me and release my hook from rocks whenever it became snagged. I finally asked him, "What's the matter with that girl? Why doesn't she go fishing or play with you?"

"The girl from Tanturah, you mean?" he asked.

He told me what he knew about her, and I learned that they always called her Tanturiyya after her village, and knew her by no other name. He related how she had been visiting her relatives in

Jisr al-Zarqa when her village fell and her own family fled. She had stayed on afterward with her mother's relatives in Jisr al-Zarqa. "She thinks of herself as a big-town girl and always lords it over us. And she's a bit funny too; she's always either smiling or crying. We don't know what to make of her, and so we keep out of her way. She's not one of us; she just reads, smiles, and cries all by herself."

When I asked the boy to find out her name and who her uncles were and to report all this back to me the following week, he returned with his friends and they all began throwing rocks at me. And after that my Tanturiyya leaned no more on her rock and I didn't dare visit that beach again.

I shut myself up in my room at the Union of Palestine Workers, feeling depressed and wondering if she would be lost to me as Yuaad had been. Then one day my master, Jacob burst in screaming, "What were you doing in Jisr al-Zarqa?"

"I was fishing there. It's a pastime of mine."

"What business, then, do you have with the village girls?"

"I didn't know she was a Communist!"

Jacob burst out laughing and I did the same. He then said that he was laughing because I was so naive. Obviously, he observed, there was no danger of any Communists appearing in that village so long as its inhabitants remained isolated by the sand, the dark of the night, and the spider's web.

"Spider's web?"

"Why, yes. They're all one family. Their family bonds tie them together like a spider's web."

"And the girl from Tanturah?"

Jacob repeated what I already knew of her origins, adding that her family had been "on our side," although he did feel uneasy about her name, which was Baqiyya, a word meaning "one who stays." "Yes," he observed, "there seems to be some contradiction there. But she's just a child."

And he promised he would get her for me if I arose before dawn, went to the workers from the villages who sleep in the slums of Haifa, and woke them up—before dawn, mind you—to the danger of the Communists. I promised him I would do this and began spending the night with them. Each morning they would leave me still sound asleep and go off to earn their living.

When the elections for the second Knesset were held, in July 1951, and the Communist party got sixteen votes in Jisr al-Zarqa, Jacob came in smiling and exclaimed, "Great news! Great news! The big man (of small stature) has decided to target you at Jisr al-Zarqa so that you can eliminate those votes."

"How?"

"By getting you married to Baqiyya!"

By the end of July, Baqiyya and I were married. No sooner were we alone together, and I began whispering endearments to her, then she burst out, "Not yet. First I want you to share my secret with me."

Twenty-seven:

Saeed Becomes Possessed of Two Secrets

That night Baqiyya told me what no bridegroom has ever heard before on his wedding night, something one cannot imagine coming from a young girl like her. She said, "Listen, husband, I really did fall in love with you. By the lives of my father and mother, I did fall for you and I do still love you. But I did not appreciate your sending those people to ask my uncle for my hand.

"And I want to tell you also, husband, that I am very young, under the legal age for marriage. But I also know that those who make the laws will ignore them if it is in their interests to do so. What exactly are they after?

"Please let me go on. I did keep on loving you until you loved me. And now here I am, your bride and your life partner, and we are going to set up a home together. My hopes are all in you, husband. Now, what I want is to return to the ruins of my village, Tanturah, and go to the beach there and its calm sea. In a cave in the rocks below, beneath the sea, there is an iron chest, full of gold, the jewelry of my grandmother, mother, and sisters, as well as my own. My father hid it there and told us about it so that any of us who ever needed it could make use of it.

"I want you, husband, to arrange it so that we can go back in secret to the shore of Tanturah; or perhaps you can return all alone and remove the chest from its hiding place. Its contents will relieve us of the poverty you suffer. I don't want my children to grow up hunchbacked from always looking down. I am used to living in freedom, husband!"

I was flabbergasted, utterly amazed, at the candor with which this girl expressed herself. Her manner and speech illuminated for me a truth about your friends, my dear sir, that would otherwise always have intrigued me: namely, how they maintain their courage in the face of officialdom and are never awed by a big man, even when not of small stature, no matter how poor they may be.

Then I realized your secret: every one of you must have an iron chest in your own Tanturah, where your father hid his treasure of gold! When I realized that through this treasure I had become one of you, without you knowing a thing about it, a great burden was lifted from my mind.

What aroused my admiration most was your ability to conceal this secret despite the fact that it must be known to thousands of you, even to tens of thousands. So I said to myself: If they can do this, why can't I? Especially since my secret was known only to the two of us, to Baqiyya and myself. I set about assuring her of both my trustworthiness and my manhood. I mixed my tears with hers, an activity even more likely to preserve marriage than the mixing of blood in the veins of children. She calmed right down, felt secure with me, and indeed became my life partner.

From that night on I began calling myself " the man with two secrets ": my secret and yours. My knowledge of your secret definitely lightened my burden, but my knowledge of Baqiyya's scared me to death.

Twenty-eight:

Saeed Becomes a "Man with a Mission"

"Get some sleep now," I told her. "Everything will clear itself up in the morning."

But I did not sleep. For I realized that our path to that treasure was fraught with danger. If I did not arrange it all most carefully, we would be ruined, neither attaining our treasure nor preserving our secret. If that house my brother had built on the shore had become property of the state of the big man, of small stature, how would it be with an iron chest in the sea only a few yards from shore and therefore most definitely within Israel's territorial waters?

Baqiyya realized as I did how dangerous it all was, critically dangerous. For she even believed, really and truly, that the Arabs who had remained in Israel were themselves also government property. She told me that it was the village chief who had told her that, and that the government had told it to him.

One night I asked her: "Didn't your uncles own land in Jisr al-Zarqa?" She replied that they did once, but that the government had confiscated it along with the rest of the land in their village.

"But didn't your uncles have recourse to the law?" I asked.

She was clearly amazed at my question and replied, "The village chief informed us how they had told him: 'You fought and were defeated; therefore both you and all your property have legally become ours. By what law do the defeated claim their rights from the conqueror?' "

"Great! Great! So that's it!" I exclaimed. "That's why the big man was so keen on preventing the Communists from entering your village and others like it isolated by nature. And if nature did not isolate them, then the government did it with barbed wire."

Immediately I wished I had not said this, for Baqiyya opened her eyes wide and rained questions down on me. "Who are the Communists?"

"Ungrateful people who deny the blessings."

"What blessings?"

"The blessings of life which victors bestow upon the conquered."

"But such blessings come from God."

"Well, they deny God. They're heretics."

"How are they heretics?"

"They claim, God preserve us from them, that they can change predetermined fate."

This explanation made her even more eager and persistent. "However could they be that powerful?" she demanded.

"Perhaps they found, as we did, chests their fathers had left for them, hidden along the beaches of their own Tanturahs."

This answer inflamed her imagination all the more. Her eyes gleamed and she knit her brows in determination and insisted, "Then we must seek help from the Communists."

I realized now that I had plunged into a bottomless well and that no matter how much I wanted to drag her out of this Communist business, the deeper I would fall into it. It disturbed me to realize that if Jacob had heard this dialogue he would have accused me of spreading Communist propaganda. I whispered to her how necessary it was to be cautious.

And since my father, God rest his soul, had left me no worldly goods at all, just my sense of caution, I set about offering this inheritance to her every morning and evening. "My father," I told her, "warned me that people eat people, so never trust those around you. You should suspect everyone, even your own brothers and sisters, from your own parents. For even if they do not in fact eat you, they could if they wished."

I lectured her endlessly on the need for circumspection and caution until she fell asleep in my arms. But I remained awake all night myself, pondering the problem of the chest and how to recover it.

Twenty-nine:

The Story of Thurayya, Who Was Reduced to Eating Mud

Now, twenty years later, when I read about that old lady Thurayya Abdel Qadir Maqbul, from Lydda, who lost her treasure because of her goodheartedness, or rather her naivete, I realize that I did well not to take chances but to protect myself from all possible dangers and surprises that might occur. That's how I've managed to keep my secret right up to now, undisclosed to anyone—except you, dear sir.

For on the tenth day of September, in the fifth year A.J.—after the June War, that is, and therefore 1971—your paper *al-Ittihad*, quoting *Maariv*, which in turn quoted *Haaretz*, which got its information from police headquarters, who themselves quoted Lydda police, reported that an old lady named Thurayya Abdel Qadir Maqbul, seventy years of age, returned from Jordan to her town and birthplace, Lydda. This was possible due to the act that permitted a summer vacation across the "open bridges." Her visit came after an absence of twenty-three years from her country; she had spent all this time as a refugee in Amman with her husband and children. They had lived in poverty in Amman until her two boys grew up and went to work in Kuwait. They returned at last clutching some of that black oil and built a house in Amman. And it was from this home that they bade farewell to their father, to his grave.

During Black September of 1970, a Hashimite tank—a "Sherman," simple and saintly—levelled that house completely. Nothing emerged from the rubble except good-hearted Thurayya, still safe and sound. Standing there amid that ruin, in the wasteland of her now barren life and quite alone in the world, she remembered her lost paradise and how glorious things had once been for her in her fine house in Lydda. She had hidden her key in one niche in the wall, and in another her jewelry. She had put her jewelry in tin boxes before she left with the refugees in 1948, confident that she would return, like all the rest, "one day soon." At last, after twenty-three years, that day had come. She decided she would go, crossed the open bridge that summer, and lost everything.

When she went to enter her old house in Lydda to retrieve her treasure, her "lawful" heiress (going back to Noah's time) slammed the door in her face. But she was not shocked—aware, as she was, that cruelty from one's own kinsmen is always more difficult to bear. Her Arab relatives in Israel advised her to seek help from the forces of law and order, from the Israeli police, that is, and she did. They sent one policeman with her, along with an official, a Custodian of Enemy Property. These two did not wish to disturb the lawful heiress, and so they approached the old lady's house from the rear, via the home of an Arab relative of hers who welcomed her warmly.

Thurayya pointed to a place in the wall; they dug and found the tin boxes with the jewelry. Then she indicated another place; they dug and found her key. How they all cheered and praised God! The eyes of all present brimmed with tears of emotion. The policeman wiped away those of the Custodian with his handkerchief; the Custodian greatly appreciated the policeman's kindness of heart and so wiped away his tears with his own handkerchief. The Arabs and the Jews hugged one another and shared tears of joy, gratitude, and a shared humanity. Then they contacted journalists who published the news, and a radio station which broadcast it. During those unforgettable days, kindergarten teachers told their children how the Israeli police search for treasures hidden by lonely Arab mothers bereaved of their sons, just as they look for lost Jewish children, and are so vigilant that they never sleep.

When, however, that unfortunate lady, Thurayya, stretched out her hand to take her wedding jewels, the Custodian of Enemy Property gave her a receipt for the gold, took it himself, and left. Thurayya took the receipt for the gold and left, across the "open bridges," to eat mud in the Wihdat refugee camp and to ask God to give long life to her kinsmen and their cousins.

As far as I'm concerned, my experience has taught me not to have confidence in others and to keep my secrets tucked away. I knew that my identity card in the Union of Palestine Workers was of no use to me except when I was of negative value to others; or rather that it was of benefit only to the big man of small stature, who was himself of benefit to no one.

Eventually I moved my belongings to a house more fit for married life, from the Wadi al-Nasnas area of Haifa, fit only for animals to live in, to Jabal Street. This move, of course, required me to pay "key money." This left me with nothing with which to hire a pack animal to move my belongings, and so I had to carry them myself. As I was moving my belongings to my new home, a car stopped nearby and evil itself emerged, produced pen and paper, and said, "We, [he was in fact alone] are from the Custodian of Enemy Property."

I produced from my hip pocket my membership card in the Union of Palestine Workers and exclaimed, "Oh, we're on your side!"

"No, no," he insisted, "I want proof that this property is yours, that you haven't stolen it."

I was at a loss as to what to do. As I slipped the card into my back pocket my trousers fell a little in the process. Since when, I wondered, did people have to carry with them proof that their furniture was not stolen? I hoisted my trousers, afraid I might have to prove ownership of them too.

"No, no," he repeated. "This furniture might well be from an Arab home."

That was true, of course.

"If so, it has become state property."

"Well, we're all that," I commented.

My furniture was saved from actually becoming state property only when we called on Jacob, who convinced the policeman that

95

I already was, in fact, state property. So I carried the furniture home. I was not fully convinced, however, that the custodian had left me in peace. After that, whenever anyone knocked at my door in the dead of night I would get up in a fright, sure he had come to get my furniture.

Moreover, after the partner of my life, Baqiyya, the girl from Tanturah, shared with me the secret of her treasure, and it thus became mine too, any knock, such as that of the son of our neighbor come to invite us to his sister's wedding, would throw us from our bed to our feet in terror, and we would whisper, "They have found out!"

Actually, however, they did not find out.

Thirty:

The Story of the Golden Fish

Baqiyya's secret having become mine as well, I became caution personified on two feet. When I realized that true caution demands walking on four feet, I began to do that too.

When Baqiyya gave birth to our son, she wanted to name him after her father, a refugee, whose name was Fathi, which means "victor." But the big man of small stature raised an eyebrow at that, and so we named him Walaa, which means "loyal."

Since I realized that birth control was a proof of loyalty, we had no more children. And whenever our secret became too heavy to bear, I declared my loyalty, whether I was asked to or not. I had regarded myself as an introvert until they sent us in a delegation to Europe and had us take along lots of *tambal* hats to present to our Jewish brothers there, along with talk of milk and honey, the marrying of spinsters, and the cure for cancer. I presented them with my shirt, pants, and all my underwear, keeping nothing hidden but my secret.

During that time I would sit alone with Baqiyya, whispering with her of how best to retrieve the treasure, until eventually we developed our own code of speech, comprehensible only to us.

Sometimes at work thoughts of my secret would intrude. At such times I felt my secret could be seen in my eyes, and so I closed them tight to keep it hidden. This happened so often that people said there must be some eye affliction running in my family.

Our conversation centered so obsessively on the maxim, "Act in haste, repent at leisure," that Walaa continued to crawl until he reached the age of four. Then, to disguise things even more, I began taking him to the beach at Tanturah and encouraging him to fish. I would sit him on a rock on the promontory, and from there he would dangle his line. I would undress and enter the sea, asking him to shout out if anyone should come. I would swim far out to the little uninhabited island that lies across from the ruins of the village. I would dive as deep as I could down into a dark cave under the rocks, in the place Baqiyya had described to me. But I found nothing except fish that flitted away and seaweed sticking to the rocks. I never dared venture far into the cave.

I would remain out there until I heard my son begin to cry, afraid at being alone, or until I heard him call out for me. Then I would swim back ashore, but usually only see lovers embracing on the beach. I would then return to the water and they would continue embracing.

Walaa asked persistently what it was I was searching for, and I would tell him it was for "the golden fish." Then I'd tell him all the *Arabian Nights* tales I recalled. And I also gave free rein to my imagination, searching busily for some treasure of gold ever since the days of our ancient ancestor, Abjar son of Abjar.

"But will you find it, father?"

"If I keep on diving and you keep the secret, we'll certainly find it."

"Has anyone ever found it, father?"

"Others definitely must have found their golden fishes."

"If we should find it, what will you do with it, father?"

"As the other have done."

"But what did they do with theirs?"

"Well, they didn't tell me their secret."

At this the boy would go back to his playing or fishing, or announce he wanted to return home, which we would soon do.

I did not realize he discussed all this with his mother until one day, as we sat on the beach at Tanturah, he suddenly asked, "Why are you scared to have people see you searching for the golden fish, father?"

"So they won't beat me to it."

"If you should find it, Father, and the government got to know of it, would they take it from us just as they did Tanturah from my grandparents?"

"Whoever put those ideas into your head, boy?"

"Mummy."

That night we argued late, Baqiyya and myself, with me trying to convince her that we should keep the treasure a secret from him. I wanted her to help me teach him to be very careful of what he said, to guard his tongue, and to speak of such things only in a whisper. Our debate went on till dawn. Then suddenly we saw him enter our room, walking on tiptoe, and placing his forefinger on his pursed lips as he whispered, "Hush! The milkwoman has arrived!"

Thirty-one:

An Odd Piece of Research on the Many Virtues of the Oriental Imagination

Oh, no, not at all, my dear sir! It wasn't this story of the golden fish, nor any other such tales from the *Arabian Nights* that caused the loss of my only son, Walaa. No; for if that suppressed "Oriental imagination" which created those superb tales were once set free, it would reach the very stars.

What do you think, for example, of that story about the peasant who wished to protect his bride from gossip and so carried her in a box on his back while, day after day, he plowed his fields? When Prince Badr al-Zaman saw him and asked him about the box, and the peasant answered him truthfully, the prince demanded to look inside it with his own two eyes. The peasant lowered the chest and opened it, only to find his wife lying there inside with that rascal Aladdin! Right there, in a box on her husband's back, mind you!

And had it not been for their "Oriental imagination," would those Arabs of yours, my dear sir, have been able to live one single day in this country? Why, when Independence Day comes each year you see the Arabs joyfully bearing the flags of the state a full week before the festivities and another week after. Arab Nazareth is decorated with flying banners more than Tel Aviv, and in the Nasnas Valley in Haifa, where poor Arabs and poor Jews have come to live like brothers, it's the Arab home, not the Jewish one next door, where you see the flags flying. The Jewish home finds it enough to be Jewish. The same goes for cars on Independence Day; you can tell the national identity of their owners by the flags they display. When I asked one of my Arab compatriots what all this showed, he answered, "Imagination, brother, imagination! Those people are Europeans, with weak imaginations. We fly the flags so that they can actually see them with their own eyes."

"Well," I asked, "why don't they fly them too?"

"Imagination again, brother. They know our Oriental imagination is very penetrating and that we can see with it what they can't. We can see the flags of the state even when folded up inside people. And didn't the late Prime Minister Eshkol try to transform the so-called military government into something that observes without itself being seen? But we could still discern it, in the orders for house arrest and in the furrows deep in our cheeks. Now that's what I call imagination!"

And how about that Arab youth who slammed into another car with his own on Lillinblum Street in Tel Aviv? Wasn't it his Oriental imagination that saved him? By getting out of his car and screaming about the other driver, "He's an Arab—an Arab!" he so engaged everyone in attacking his victim that he himself was able to escape.

And don't forget Shlomo in one of Tel Aviv's very best hotels. Isn't he really Sulaiman, son of Munirah, from our own quarter? And "Dudi," isn't he really Mahmud? "Moshe," too; isn't his proper name Musa, son of Abdel Massih? How could they earn a living in a hotel, restaurant, or filling station without help from their Oriental imagination, the same imagination that gave them the story of the golden fish, and the magnetic mountain deep in the raging sea where you can never manage to get your boat unless you abstain from mention of God, no matter how high the waves nor how violent the storms?

Was it anything but the *Arabian Nights* that saved the tiny, peaceful village near West Baqah, in the "Little Triangle" of land between Israel and Jordan? During the third elections, you remember, the government went there and ordered the villagers to prevent the Communists by force from holding a meeting there; if they failed they would find themselves evicted across the border. Jacob sent me to the village an hour before the meeting was scheduled in order to investigate the situation and make sure the orders were carried out. No one was to be seen. I wandered from house to house and saw that all the doors were wide open. I went inside some, but all I saw were a few chickens running loose and some dogs lazing in the afternoon sun.

I walked on and on in a daze, feeling rather like Prince Musa in the *Arabian Nights* tale "The City of Brass." When he entered that town he found it devoid of sound and with no living creatures, "but owls hooting in the distance, hawks circling above, and crows screeching in lamentation for those who used to live there."

I wandered on until I heard the sound of coughing coming from one of the mud houses. I went inside and found a blind old cripple. When he heard me enter, he said, "Did you come then, Commies?"

"Yes, it's us," I lied. "We've come. Where are all the villagers?"

"They've all left, gone to a hill a little way off, so that neither your evil, nor that of the rulers will afflict this village. Go away, my son, why don't you, all of you, so that they can come back!"

When I asked him what had happened, he told me the villagers had held a meeting, discussed the situation, and reached a consensus, "We don't know those Commies, nor do they know us," it was agreed. "There's no hatred, no blood feuds between us. If the governor wants them dead, then he—not us—should kill them. Anyway, he is more capable of doing it than we are. But if we don't kill them, then the governor will kill us." So it was decided that they would simply abandon the village for the entire day.

"As for me," the old man added, "I stayed on because blindness has already put me out of it. I can neither kill nor be killed. So just go away, lad; just let the day pass peacefully."

I reported this good news to Jacob, but he screamed in my face, "Ass! They outwit us and you think it is good news? We wanted there to be bad blood between them, not mere distance, not just a hill!"

I had not, in fact, regarded it as good news, but I wanted him to think that I did. All the time I was having the same thoughts that must have gone through Prince Musa's mind as he read the words carved on a marble slab in that dead city of brass: "Where are they now who ruled the country, humiliated the people, and led the armies? God, who brings all pleasure to an end, sets communities asunder, and devastates prosperous homes, has come down upon them and removed them from their great palaces and placed them in narrow graves." And on a second slab there were the words: "Where now are the kings who built Iraq and ruled the world around? Where are they who built Isfahan and the lands of Khurasan? The Messenger of Death summoned them and they answered his call. The Herald of Destruction beckoned them and they responded. Nothing of all they had built, all they had established, availed them. None of what they had collected and hoarded saved them."

I, however, was not weeping as Prince Musa had done. I felt somewhat dazed, as I once did when on an errand at the military court in Nazareth. A boy of about ten came rushing out into the hallway in obvious fear and confusion and began asking some men there questions. They pointed to me. Then the child came up to me and said, "The judge wants you."

I hurried into the court holding my head high, proud that the judge wanted me, and found the court in session. Then I heard the boy say, "This, Your Honor, is one of my relatives." I was dumbfounded. The judge sentenced me on the spot to three months in prison or the payment of fifty pounds. Why? Because the child who claimed to be a relative of mine had travelled to Haifa without a military permit; and, since the rules of democracy prohibit imprisonment of a child, they decided to imprison me instead. This actually happened, on November 3, 1952.

When I denied that he was related to me, the judge delivered a lecture to those in court expressing the hope of the state that its Arab citizens would gain a sense of moral courage. He also emphasized that the state respects most those who do not deny their blood ties. When I produced my card of membership in the Union of Palestine Workers, he berated me and said, "I shall refer this matter to your superiors and have them teach you some courage!"

So I paid the fifty pounds and left, a courageous man. On the way out I looked for the boy, "my relative," and found him among some men, acting quite as though he were one of them. They laughed at me and said, "Imagination, my dear sir! That's imagination for you!"

The imagination of my only son, Walaa, however, found quite a different outlet.

Thirty-two:

An Event More Difficult to Believe Than Death Itself

My wife and I were so preoccupied with preserving our secret and with searching for the treasure deep in its hiding place below the seabed that we somewhat neglected our son, Walaa, as he was growing up.

By the time he was a young man, his behavior was certainly strange. He spoke only when necessary, and when he did say something he scattered his words here and there, like clouds in a summer sky, their shape now reminding you of an animal's head, now of horsemen attacking, and now of an angel lying prostrate.

Then came the ill-fated day of that last autumn, in 1966, before that everlasting autumn of the June War. All of a sudden an uproar of noise and movement came at me from all sides. Soldiers came bursting into my office, their weapons drawn. At their head was the big man; he had removed his dark glasses, and his face looked blacker than pitch. He was positively shaking with rage. My master Jacob stood behind him, his head lowered. All around and behind them stood soldiers. Shock had me riveted to my seat; I thought doomsday must have come.

My eyes swam. I saw rows and rows of heads all close together, dancing on the walls and floor of the room. These heads somehow seemed to be slipping out and away from my paralyzed fingers, where my hands rested on the table. These heads had their mouths gaping open and they were all screaming Arabic cusswords, but in a style not familiar to the language. This was all so funny that I had to laugh, and this led to more and more laughter until I lost control completely and my sides felt like collapsing. I regained control only when they jumped on me and threw me to the ground unconscious.

I remained in a kind of stupor while they tried to jolt my already disordered mind with a tale more difficult to believe than death is for those still alive. Walaa, my only son, that shy, skinny young man, whose dinner any cat could steal, had become a *fedaiy*, a .guerrilla, and had taken up arms in rebellion against the state! And I, so they said, was responsible for all this, along with that poisonous snake, the woman from Tanturah, who should have been made to leave along with the rest of her family. My master was also being blamed, Jacob, that ass whose Oriental greed for my Oriental food had blinded him to his duty of vigilance. No doubt, we had all conspired together, "All of you, all of you, against *me*," screamed the big man of small stature. "You planned this to destroy me: but I shall destroy you!" The state, he added, knew exactly how to preserve its security and to clamp down until its enemies were sorry they had ever been born.

I was able to assemble, between one curse and the next, and in my ongoing stupor, the threads of a tale far stranger than those stories of giants, jinn, and spirits, all about the life of my only son, Walaa.

He, along with two of his schoolmates, had founded a secret cell. Then he had retrieved, from a cave in a deep hollow in the rocks off the deserted beach of Tanturah, a well-made strongbox, shut tight so that no moisture could penetrate it. It was filled with weapons and gold.

"Baqiyya! Oh, Baqiyya! Didn't we agree not to tell him?"

"But Saeed, Saeed, our children are our only hope!"

The story went on that the boys had bought weapons, ammunition, and explosives with the gold and had established a hideout and storage depot in the basement of one of the uninhabited ruins of Tanturah. They had then sent one of their cell to Lebanon to contact the guerrillas there. But, as the big man said, the authorities had grabbed him easily enough, along with the third member of the group. Walaa took refuge in their basement hideout and was now resolved to die a martyr rather than surrender.

"So, out of compassion for you and his mother, we have come to you, Saeed Pessoptimist, to get you to go and persuade him to abandon this adolescent death wish of his. If you hadn't been one of our men, we never would have come. We want to do you a favor since you've done some for us. Get up, go home, and get his mother; then both of you proceed to the ruins of Tanturah before your lives become one big ruin. If he surrenders, we will spare his life for your sake. But if he refuses and insists on causing us a scandal, you all will die."

Since my shock was still so great that I couldn't stand, they carried me out. Baqiyya forced herself to come with us, suppressing her tears. I refrained from blaming her openly because I still wanted to preserve our secret. Finally they threw us down on the beach at Tanturah and the soldiers went a little way off.

The sun was going down. The twilight sky of evening seemed to bend down low around us in its compassion.

107

Thirty-three:

The Ultimate Tale—of the Fish That Understand All Languages

The events of that autumn evening at the deserted shore of Tanturah have remained a closely guarded state secret right up to the present. However, I don't expect they will prevent you from making it known, bearing in mind all that has happened since the June War.

I don't know what their archives show as having happened that evening. But what I have recorded within myself, and shall never forget in any detail, is the following.

When we stood before that cellar where they said Walaa was hiding, with all his weapons and explosives, Baqiyya told us, "Leave him to me; I am his mother. I not only gave him birth, but also I gave him my secret and my hope to bear himself."

I walked a little way away and sat on the remains of a wall, staring out at the calm sea but aware of nothing. How much a stranger, how very alone, I felt there in the setting sun.

His mother cautiously approached the cellar and called out, "Walaa! Walaa! Don't shoot, my son! It's your mother!"

There was silence.

"There's no point in resistance. They know everything."

Then his voice reached us, sounding curiously hoarse from the depth of the cellar. As usual, he was talking only because circumstances demanded it.

"How?"

"It was they who led me to your hiding place."

"I'm not hiding, mother. I've taken up arms only because I got sick and tired of your hiding."

Once more silence.

Then his voice again arose from the depths of the cellar. I wondered how that scrawny chest of his could hold so deep a voice.

"Woman, you up there. Who are you?"

"Your mother, Walaa. Would a son deny his mother?"

"Would my mother come with them?"

"They sent me with your father, Walaa, just the two of us, alone. He's over there, sitting on an old wall, waiting for his son to be saved."

"Then why doesn't he speak?"

"He's not very good with words."

I cleared my throat, audibly.

"Why did you come, mother?"

"They want me to persuade you to lay down your arms and come out to us; then you'll be safe."

"Why?"

"They say they want to be merciful to your father and me."

"That's very funny! So now they speak of mercy! What will happen, then, when the bullets begin to fly?"

The soldiers could be heard clearing their throats ominously.

"They'll have mercy on no one, my son."

"You're afraid of them, then?"

"It's for you I'm afraid, Walaa." Silence returned and then she pleaded once more: "Lay down your arms, Walaa, my son, and come on out."

"You, woman, who came with them, you tell me where I should come."

"Out into the open air, my son. That cellar is too small, too shut in. You'll suffocate down there."

"Suffocate? It was to breathe free that I came to this cellar, to breathe in freedom just once. In my cradle you stifled my crying. As I grew and tried to learn how to talk from what you said, I heard only whispers.

"As I went to school you warned me, 'Careful what you say!' When I told you my teacher was my friend, you whispered, 'He may be spying on you.' When I heard what had happened to Tanturah and cursed them, you murmured, 'Careful what you say.' When they cursed me, you repeated, 'Careful what you say.' When I met with my schoolmates to announce a strike, they told me, 'Careful what you say.'

"One morning you told me, mother, 'You talk in your sleep; careful what you say in your sleep!' I used to sing in the bath, but Father would shout at me, 'Change that tune! The walls have ears. Careful what you say!'

" 'Careful what you say!' 'Careful what you say!' Always 'Careful what you say!' Just for once, just once, I want to be careless about what I say.

"I was suffocating! This may be a poky little cellar, Mother, but there's more room here than you have ever had! Shut in it may be, but it's also a way out!"

Silence again. Then we heard the clanking of guns being readied.

His mother cried out; "A way out? How? Death is no way out, merely an end. There's no shame in how we live. If we are secretive, it's only in hope of deliverance. If we're 'careful,' it's only to protect all of you. Where's the shame in you coming out to us, Walaa, to your father and mother? Alone you have power over nothing."

"I do have power over you."

"But we aren't your enemies."

"You are not on my side, either."

"Son, do be careful!"

"Oh yes, very funny! Say it again, mother, 'Careful what you say.' I am free now."

"Free? I thought you were bearing arms to take your freedom."

Again there was silence, broken by her sarcastic laugh and comment: "If only we were free, my son, we wouldn't quarrel. You'd not bear arms and we'd not ask you to be 'careful.' We act this way because we do seek freedom."

"How?"

"As nature seeks its freedom. Dawn rises only after night has

110

completed its term. The lily buds only when its bulb is ripe. Nature is averse to abortion, my son. And the people aren't ready to face what you're about to do."

"I shall bear the burden for them until they are ready."

"My son! My son! Nothing is lovelier than a rose in a young man's lapel. But the mother rose can give it no more nourishment then! Oh, let me hug you close to me!"

Silence again. Then I heard him moan: "Mother, mother, how long must we wait for the lilies to bud?"

"Don't think of it as waiting, son. We must simply plow and plant and bear our burden until it is harvest time."

"When will the harvest be ready?"

"Just stick it out."

"All my life I've 'stuck it out.' "

"Stick it out some more."

"I'm sick of your submissiveness!"

"But there are some young men and women among us who have resisted. Be like them! They bore the burden of the longest night and carried the burning sun on their foreheads, and the only way the authorities could force them from the land was by putting them in jail. And the government couldn't demolish their houses over them without also destroying one of their very own myths. But you have given up hope, son."

"Darkness is all I see around me."

"Only in that cellar."

"My whole life has been inside a cellar."

"But you're still within the bulb, waiting to bud. Come up to the light of the sun!"

"Where is my 'place in the sun'?"

"In the sun. Everything will work itself out. Look how many peoples have seized their freedom. Our season will come yet."

"Must you keep dreaming about the seven islands behind the seven lakes?"

"They're our islands and our lakes, Walaa. Sinbad has ended his voyages and has begun seeking treasures in the soil of his own country."

"His life in his land is unbearable."

111

"When life becomes cheaper than death, then holding on to it by our very teeth becomes more difficult than giving it up."

"Mother, you will die without your own people returning."

"*Before* my people return, you mean!"

"How?"

"Time! Let time do its work."

His sarcastic laugh reverberated from the cellar. "Time itself will kill you who gave me life and me too."

"Don't speak lightly of time, Walaa. Without time no plant would grow and we could not eat. The sun would not rise after night and no peace would come after war."

"But has it come?"

"It will. And without time no prisoner would ever be released."

"Have any been?"

"They will be. And without time experience would not give people lessons from which to learn."

"But have they learned any lessons?"

"You want one generation to resolve the issue?"

"Yes, my generation."

"Why yours?"

"Because it is *my* generation."

"With what weapons does your generation fight?"

There was silence again. Finally I heard her ask, in the same tone that she would request, when he was still a child, a kiss, "What kind of weapon do you have in your hands now, Walaa?"

"An old machine gun from the chest."

Suddenly I saw her make a dash for the cellar, her arms stretched out at her sides, like a mother bird speeding to her nest to protect her young. She seemed about to disappear into the dark opening but he cried out to her and stopped her.

"They're advancing behind you, mother. Would you protect them with your love for me?"

"No, Walaa, my son, I just want to join you. There's another machine gun in the chest. I'll use my love to protect you."

No sooner had she disappeared from my sight than chaos broke out. I could no longer distinguish among the many figures dashing all around, ignoring me completely. I heard only muffled shouts and

112

orders being given. I advanced, retreated, and wandered around in circles. I heard curses too, but not directed at me.

A kind of a dream sequence followed. With all the stars now set and the moon's face dark, I made out figures racing for the sea. I heard splashes and felt water spatter me. Then I heard someone say, "They dived into the water, over here!"

Another voice then arose: "No, it was over here!"

I could not see the big man but could hear him ordering them not to shoot but to dive into the water after them. I was not there when they finally brought the searchlights and the frogmen, for my master Jacob, standing at my side, took my arm and drove me home in his car, to my empty house.

Next day he visited me and ordered me to keep secret all that had happened. If I did so they would pardon me and permit me to return to work.

"After you have killed them both?" I asked.

Then he told me to my amazement—and I did not know whether to believe him or not—that they had managed to escape completely, without a trace.

They had been last seen going toward the sea, mother and son, she embracing him and he supporting her, until they had disappeared into the water. The soldiers, he said, had been taken by surprise, and the big man had forbidden them to shoot to keep the news from spreading. He was sure they would either be caught or drown. However, the day and night search for them had not found them alive, nor had their bodies been discovered. Their fate remains a closely guarded state secret, too.

Over the next few days Jacob displayed great sympathy for me, but I did not want to tell him what I knew of the cave deep in the rock on the sea bottom. I believed my wife and son had decided to go there to die.

How often I felt an urge to go down to find out for myself, but I didn't have the heart for it. To preserve a spark of hope that they were still alive was better than to drown it.

But I did start going back to the beach at Tanturah, now crowded with bathers, and would sit on the rocky promontory there, as Walaa had done, and lower my fishing line, mouthing a silent call to my son, hoping always for some response.

One day a Jewish boy who had sat down unnoticed beside me surprised me with the question, "In what language are you speaking, Uncle?"

"In Arabic."

"With whom?"

"With the fish."

"Do the fish understand only Arabic?"

"Yes, the old fish, the ones that were here when the Arabs were."

"And the young fish, do they understand Hebrew?"

"They understand Hebrew, Arabic, and all languages. The seas are wide and flow together. They have no borders and have room enough for all fish."

"Wow!"

The boy's father called him and he hurried away. I heard them speaking and smiled back at them. The child seemed to think I was King Solomon, and I saw them gesturing in my direction. His father smiled and they came over toward me. The child clearly felt great respect for me and insisted on staying beside me for a while. I gave him a little fish. He talked to it but it did not respond. I told him, "It's still too young." He threw it back in so that it could grow and learn how to speak. I said to myself, If only people could remain as children. Then Walaa would not have grown up and I would not have lost him. Why even the big man must have been a child once!

For several months I lived in certainty that I would receive some sign from them. At any knock on my door I would jump up at once, excited that it might mean a message from them. And after I learned that among the guerrilla units there was one named after Tanturah, I began shutting my windows and stretching out on my bed, hugging my transistor radio.

Finally along came June 5, 1967, and during its long night I heard from below shouts of "Put out that light! Put out that light!"

Extinguish it I did, but sleep I did not.

114

BOOK THREE:
THE SECOND YUAAD

How I have yearned to hear ululations
Of women burdened by a thousand years
Of longing for song and celebration.

SAMIH SABBAGH
AL-BUQAI'AH

Thirty-four:

Saeed Finds Himself Sitting on a Stake

This time Saeed Pessoptimist wrote to me as follows:

The end came when I awoke after one interminable night and found myself not in my bed. I felt chilly. When I stretched out my hand for a cover I grasped nothing but a void.

I found myself sitting on a flat surface, cold and round, not more than a yard across. A wind was blowing, strong and bitter cold, and my legs seemed to be dangling over the side of a fathomless pit. I wanted to rest my back but found that there was a pit behind me like the one in front, and that it surrounded me on all sides. If I moved, I would be certain to fall. I realized that I was sitting on the top of a blunt stake.

I shouted, "Help!" But only an echo responded, its every letter clear. I then realized that I was sitting at a dizzy height. I tried to alleviate my anxiety by chatting with the echo. This conversation was quite entertaining and finally the chasm beneath me gave a smile of dawn, even if it looked somewhat stern with all the dust.

What was I to do?

Well, I said to myself, don't be such a worry-wart. Busy your brain box, why don't you. Now, whatever could have placed you in such a situation? Is it reasonable for you to have gone to sleep one night in your own bed and then to wake up on top of a stake?

The laws of both nature and logic disallow this. You must therefore be in a dream, even if it's an unusually long one.

So why am I still sitting here on this stake, being bumped and buffeted by the cold, without a cover, back support, or companion. Why don't I go down? This stake business must be a nightmare. If I descend from the stake I will no doubt shake off the dream completely and get back to bed, where I'll be able to cover myself up and feel warm. Why hesitate? For fear of falling from my enormous height down into the depths below, like a duck killed by a hunter, to suffer pain and to die?

It is all clearly imaginary, both my position and the stake too. It is all a typical dream, a contradiction of the laws of nature and the rules of logic. Come now, grip the stake with your legs and arms and, with all the strength, fortitude, and will power you can muster under pressure, descend it slowly, like a squirrel.

So I dropped my dangling legs over, feeling the surface of the stake. But it was smooth and cold, like the skin of a snake, and I realized that I would not be able to keep a grip on it. I was sure that if I tried to climb down, I would fall into the pit, break my neck, suffer pain, and die. I therefore stopped.

Then I remembered those Indian magicians who send up a rope far into the air until its end disappears into the clouds. The magician climbs it until he too is lost to sight. Then he climbs down, not only without any harm befalling him but making his fortune in the process. However, I was no Indian magician, just an Arab who had remained, by some magic, in Israel.

I felt like shouting, "I am having a nightmare!" and then jumping. I couldn't simply stay there to die.

Well, I did shout but did not jump. For if my position and the stake were merely imaginary, and I was only having a nightmare, it would not last long whether I jumped or remained seated. I was undoubtedly about to awake, to discover myself in my bed, warm and well covered. So what need did I have to race the hours, and maybe even the minutes or seconds, to that moment of reawakening which was certainly approaching?

Why should I jump if remaining seated would lead me to the same result?

Then a great shudder at the cold shook me and would have thrown me from the stake were it not for an irresistible counter-shudder that occurred as a thought struck me.

What if this were all true, not a dream or nightmare? To say that it all contradicted the laws of nature and the rules of logic was no proof that it was not true. Had not my own family, the Pessoptimists, searched for happiness over the centuries in miracles that contradicted these laws? My ancestors kept on breaking their necks searching the ground at their feet for buried treasure, and I too had found what I had sought so long by gazing above my head and discovering my brothers from outer space who had restored my calm. Why should I be expected, alone among all my fathers and grandfathers, as I sat there on that stake, to submit my fate to the laws of nature and the rules of logic?

So I remained in this state, shaking between one shudder and another, the cold pushing me and my pride in my great ancestry pulling me, until I met Yuaad once again and felt warm for the first time in a thousand years.

Thirty-five:

A Flag of Surrender, Flying on a Broomstick, becomes a Banner of Revolt against the State

I met Yuaad where meetings in Israel often occur—in prison. Actually, I was on my way out of prison at the time. I got there in the first place when I overdid my loyalty bit, so that the authorities saw it as disloyalty.

It all came about on one of those devil-ridden nights of the June War. I was tuned in, to be on the safe side, to the Arabic-language broadcast of Radio Israel. I heard the announcer calling upon the "defeated Arabs" to raise white flags on the roofs of their homes so that the Israeli servicemen, flashing about arrow-quick all over the place, would leave them alone, sleeping safe and sound inside.

This order somewhat confused me: to which "defeated Arabs" was the announcer referring? Those defeated in this war or those defeated by the treaty of Rhodes? I thought it would be safe to regard myself as one of those "defeated" and convinced myself that if I was making a mistake, they would interpret it as an innocent one. So I made a white flag from a sheet, attached it to a broomstick, and raised it above the roof of my house in Jabal Street in Haifa, an extravagant symbol of my loyalty to the state.

But who, one might ask, was I trying to impress? As soon as my flag was flying for all to see, my master Jacob honored me by bursting in on me, without so much as a "How are you?" So I did not greet him either.

He yelled, "Lower it, you mule!"

I lowered my head until it touched his very feet and asked, "Did they appoint you King of the West Bank, Your Majesty?"

Jacob seized me by the lapels of my pajamas and began pushing me up the stairs towards the roof, repeating, "The sheet, the sheet!" When we reached the broomstick he grabbed it, and I thought he wanted to beat me with it. So we fought over it, as if doing the stick dance together, until finally he collapsed at the edge of the roof.

He began to weep, saying, "You're finished, old friend of a lifetime; you're finished and so am I along with you."

I tried to explain: "But I raised the sheet on the broomstick in response to the Radio Israel announcer."

"Ass! Ass!" he responded.

"How is it my fault if he's an ass?" I asked. "And why do you only employ asses as announcers?"

He then made it clear that I was the ass to whom he had referred. He also pointed out that all Radio Israel's announcers are Arabs; they must have worded the request badly, he commented, but I must still be a fool to have misunderstood it.

In defense of my own people, the Arabs who worked at the radio station, I said, "The duty of a messenger is to deliver the message. They say only what is dictated to them. If raising a white flag on a broomstick is an insult to the dignity of surrender, it's only because broomsticks are the only weapons you permit us.

"However," I continued, "if, since the outbreak of this war, they too have become some kind of deadly white weapon we are not permitted to carry without a permit, like the shotguns only village chiefs and old men who've spent all their lives serving the state are permitted to carry, then I'm with you as always, all the way. You know full well, old friend of a lifetime, of my extravagant loyalty to the state, to its security and its laws, whether promulgated or still to be so."

My friend Jacob, standing there with his mouth open and listening to my gabbling, was unable to stop the tears pouring down his cheeks or my raving.

Finally he regained his composure and explained how my "misunderstanding" had been considered something quite different by the big man, nothing less than a case of rebellion against the state.

"But it's only a broomstick," I objected.

"That announcer," he emphasized, "was telling the West Bank Arabs to raise white flags in surrender to the Israeli occupation. What did you think you were up to, doing that in the very heart of the state of Israel, in Haifa, which no one regards as a city under occupation?"

"But you can't have too much of a good thing," I pointed out.

"No," he insisted, "it's an indication that you do regard Haifa as an occupied city and are therefore advocating its separation from the state."

"That interpretation never so much as crossed my mind."

"We don't punish you for what crosses your minds but for what crosses the big man's mind. He considers the white flag you raised over your house in Haifa to be proof that you are engaged in combat against the state and that you do not recognize it."

"But," I objected, you know full well that I serve the security of the state to my utmost and would never do anything to harm it."

"The big man has come to believe that the extravagance of your loyalty is only a way of concealing your disloyalty. He recalls your parentage and character and regards them as proof that you only pretend to be a fool. If you are innocent, why was it 'Yuaad' you loved, 'Baqiyya' you married, and 'Walaa' you had as a son? All these names are highly suspect to the state."

"Has the big man ever stopped to ask why I was born only an Arab and could have only this as my country?"

"Come along and ask him yourself."

But instead they took me to the Bisan Depression and imprisoned me in the awesome Shatta jail.

122

Thirty-six:

A Shattering Conversation on the Road to Shatta Prison

The big man insisted on accompanying me to jail to hand me over personally to the warden. Those such as myself, inherited by the state from our own fathers, remain high in status even in prison. We are like nobles; out of favor at court, we will be dispatched to temporary exile on one of the nicer islands.

At least that's what I told myself as they squeezed me among six policemen in the back of the police van, the big man sitting in front with the large driver. It seemed like a dog-catcher's van, in the back. When they closed the door, I told myself that it was done to preserve my good reputation. When they grumbled at the extreme heat—it was August—I complained along with them. But when they pounced on me and began kicking and beating me, I yelled, "Help! Help, O, big man!" I pronounced this phrase in high Hebrew to convince them of my status and to get them to stop. The van did stop.

I found that we were then at a crossroad between Nazareth and Nahlal, passing the plain of Ibn Amir. The big man signalled to the policemen through the glass window separating him from "the dogs." They led me out and stuffed me in between the big man and the driver. I made myself comfortable and sighed, breathed the fresh air deep, and remarked, "Oh, I see we're in the plain of Ibn Amir."

Obviously annoyed, he corrected me: "No, it's the Yizrael plain!"

" 'What's in a name?' as Shakespeare put it," I soothed him.

I spoke the line in English, causing him to murmur, "Oh, so you quote Shakespeare, do you?"

I smiled, relaxing. But I noticed that the big man was growling ominously under his breath. Had I known what this implied, I'd have been better off keeping my knowledge of Shakespeare within my heart rather than quoting him by heart.

As we descended further down into the plain toward its city of Affulah, with the hills of Nazareth to our left, the big man began reciting to me the principles governing my new life in prison, the etiquette of behavior toward the jailers who were my superiors and the other inmates who were my inferiors. He promised, moreover, to get me promoted to a liaison position.

While he was going through these lessons, I became ever more certain that what is required of us inside prison is no different from what is required of us on the outside. My delight at this discovery was so great that I exclaimed joyfully, "Why, God bless you, sir!"

He went on, "If a jailer should call you, your first response must be: 'Yes sir!' And if he should tell you off, you must reply: 'At your command, sir!' And if you should hear your fellow inmates engaging in any conversation that threatens the security of the prison, even by implication, you must inform the warden. Now if he should give you a beating, then say—"

I interrupted him with the proper response, "That's your right, sir!"

"How did you know that? Were you ever imprisoned before?"

"Oh, no. God forbid, sir, that anyone should have beaten you to this favor! I have merely noticed according to your account of prison rules of etiquette and behavior that your prisons treat inmates with great humanitarianism and compassion—just as you treat us on the outside. And we behave the same, too. But how do you punish Arabs who are criminals, sir?"

"This bothers us considerably. That's why our minister general has said that our occupation has been the most compassionate known

124

on earth ever since Paradise was liberated from its occupation by Adam and Eve.

"Among our leadership there are some who believe that we treat Arabs inside prisons even better than we treat them outside, though this latter treatment is, as you know, excellent. These same leaders are convinced that we thus encourage them to continue to resist our civilizational mission in the new territories, just like those ungrateful African cannibals who eat their benefactors."

"How do you mean, sir?"

"Well, take for example our policy of punishing people with exile. This we award them without their going to jail. If they once entered jail, they would become as firmly established there as the British occupation once was."

"Yes, God bless you indeed, sir!"

"And we demolish their homes when they're outside, but when they're inside prison we let them occupy themselves building."

"That's really great! God bless you! But what do they build?"

"New prisons and new cells in old jails; and they plant shade trees around them too."

"God bless you again! But why do you demolish their homes outside the prisons?"

"To exterminate the rats that build their nests in them. This way we save them from the plague."

"God bless and save you! But could you explain that?"

"This was the justification, pure and humanitarian, made by the Ministry of Health, and quoted by the minister of defense when he explained the reasons compelling us to demolish the houses in the Jiftlick villages in the lowlands. That was the response he gave to the accusations thrown in our faces in the Knesset by that Jewish Communist congressman, that stooge of Nasser, King Husain, the Emir of Kuwait, and Shaikh Qabus!"

"And was he shut up?"

"Actually, they really screwed him."

"How, exactly?"

"The speaker prevented him from continuing his speech. Democracy is not mere chaos, my boy. Now the Communists, as you know, are chaos mongers. Their representative refused to obey the rules of democracy, and the speaker had him forcibly ejected from the sitting. That screwed him, alright!"

By now the police car was leaving the city of Affulah on the Bisan road, which led to my new residence. On both sides refreshing water was being sprayed on to the green vegetation, fresh in the very heart of summer. Suddenly the big man, cramped there with me and the driver in the front seat of that dogcart, was transformed into a poet.

While I sat there being my usual Pessoptimistic self, he was ecstatic: "Verdant fields! Green on your right and on your left; green everywhere! We have given life to what was dead. This is why we have named the borders of former Israel the Green Belt. For beyond them lie barren mountains and desert reaches, a wilderness calling out to us, 'Come ye hither, tractors of civilization!'

"If you had been with me, boy, when we crossed the Latrun road on our way to Jerusalem, you would really have seen the Green Belt: the greenery of our pine-clad hills, trees everywhere hugging one another, branch intertwined with branch, while lovers embraced beneath them. Then you would have seen, facing these green-robed hills, your barren mountains devoid of any cover that could hide their naked rocks. There they remained, weeping for a quarter of a century, shedding all their earth. Let us wipe the tears dry while you weep away, building your palaces on the rock above."

"Was this why you demolished the Latrun villages, Imwas, Yalu, and Bait Nuba, and drove their inhabitants away, master?"

"But we gave the monastery to the monks, for a tourist attraction. And we left the graveyards to those buried there, out of our faith in God. These great expanses, however, are ours, our inheritance from the war. 'Let bygones be bygones.' That's an American proverb, of German origin."

As he reached this point in his poetic discourse, the car was nearing the ancient dwellings of Ain Jalut, a village that now bears its biblical name, Ain Harud. There a spring flows into a pool constructed by the kibbutzers; this is frequented by the people of Nazareth, who go there to freshen up and curse the Mongols.

I felt like matching his poetic display, but he discouraged me, saying, "You defeated the Mongols in the battle of Ain Jalut because they had come only to loot and leave; but we loot and stay, and it is you who will go. Don't bother yourself with all those whisperings about history. Prepare to enter Shatta prison."

Immediately after he had spoken these words, a sudden change in the face of the countryside around us took place. In an instant the greenery disappeared and the eye could see only barren land and rugged rocks, to the right, the left and straight ahead. It was as if the backdrop in a theater had been changed.

Feigning ignorance of geopolitics, I commented sarcastically, "So now we have left the Green Belt and have entered the Dust Bowl of the Arabs, who have let their lands go to waste."

He scolded me, shouting, "I used to think you were a cretin, but now I find you are a pinko red! Look ahead and see where you're going!"

I looked before me and saw a huge building towering like an ugly demon of the desert; its walls were yellow, and around it there was a high, white outer wall. There were guards posted on each of the four sides of the roof, and they could be seen standing with their guns at the ready. We were awestruck by the spectacle of this yellow castle, so exposed and naked of any vegetation, protruding like a cancerous lump on the breast of a land itself sick with cancer. The big man was unable to control himself and exclaimed, "There! The terrible Shatta prison! How fantastic!"

I stretched my neck forward in alarm and whispered, "God bless us all!"

This led him to comment, "It is the prison warden who will bless you. Come on down. I'll ask him to look after you."

Thirty-seven:

How Saeed Finds Himself in the Midst of an Arabian-Shakespearean Poetry Circle

We got out of the van in front of the iron gates of the jail. The soldiers also alighted from the dog cart; three of them approached and put me under close guard. The big man himself headed the procession. He knocked just once. A dog barked inside and the gate opened.

There was the prison warden himself, mind you, in the flesh—and he had lots of it—preceded by his pet bulldog, coming forward to meet us. The master smiled welcomingly while the dog growled. The big man and the fat warden played with the dog awhile, patted him, then climbed a flight of stairs, while I remained standing in the inner courtyard surrounded by the soldiers.

Eventually one of the soldiers ordered me to go with him, and we climbed some stairs to a corridor, then to another and then another. At last we reached the warden's office, where we found the two men sipping coffee with audible pleasure.

The warden smiled at me and said, "On the recommendation of my dear friend, the big man, I shall give you special treatment. I have learned from him that your past is as white as snow, without so much as one black mark except that of the white flag. He has told me, moreover, that you're an educated lad and quote from Shakespeare."

This made me feel most relaxed, and I settled comfortably into a chair.

He promptly offered me coffee and conversation on Shakespeare. He began quoting from Anthony's speech over the body of Caesar, with me filling in the lines he had forgotten, while he exclaimed, "Oh, bravo! Bravo!"

Then he stood up and began acting the role of Othello giving Desdaemona the fatal kiss. I stretched out on the ground like her, but he said, "Get up! It's not time for that yet!" I did get up, but I was beginning to feel a little uneasy.

"However," he explained, "in the presence of the other prisoners we shall treat you as we do them. You understand, naturally."

"Yes, I understand, sir!" I glanced over at the big man reassuringly, and he returned my look in even greater measure.

The warden pressed a button and a guard entered. I shook hands with the warden, then with the big man. I asked him to look after Jacob for me. I kept on thanking this one and praising that one until the guard pushed me out of the office. As we penetrated the length of the second corridor, I said to myself, this guard is my friend, my brother; we have walked together along two corridors in the same prison. It is like sharing bread and salt. I commented: "What a highly cultured warden."

"What were you speaking about?" he asked.

"Oh, about Shakespeare and Othello and Desdemona."

"You know them then?"

"I quote from the first and lie down like the third."

"Good for you."

Then he led me into a dark room with no windows or furniture. When he switched on an overhead electric light, I found myself standing in the middle of a circle of jailers, all tall and broad shouldered. Each one had sleepy eyes, arms at the ready with sleeves rolled up, thick, strong legs, and a mouth wearing a smile worse than a frown. They all seemed to have been formed in the same mold.

I tried my best to carve on my own mouth that same smile, but the left side of my face kept collapsing and when I corrected it the right would promptly collapse. Having corrected that, I would feel my lower lip give way, and when I would repair that my teeth would chatter.

While I was engrossed in this labial exercise, I heard the guard who had led me to this nightmarish room tell the thick-thighed jailers, "And he quotes from Shakespeare, too!"

This was the signal for the beginning of a literary competition the likes of which the entire history of the literature of the Arabs since pre-Islamic times has never recorded.

One of them began with the comment, "Quote some Shakespeare for us, you son of a bitch!" Then he gave me a tremendous punch.

Another jailer caught me and said, "Here, take this, Caesar!"

I tottered toward first one jailer and then another until they got bored with punching me and began kicking me. Then I rolled around at their feet as they booted me again and again. At times I was quicker than them, but then I would feel several feet trampling on me all together. I screamed but could hear nothing, just stifled noises coming from the beating, kicking, and punching. Then I could no longer feel the blows but could only sense them faintly, as if they came from somewhere far away. They had stopped repeating verses from Shakespeare and were concentrating on the poetry of sighs and moans, with them sighing at this display of their strength and me moaning in exhaustion. I kept up this moaning as they did their sighing until I felt their boots cutting off my breath, and I sank down unconscious, completely defeated.

The last thing I heard them say was, "Welcome a thousand times, our very own Shakespeare!" This nickname stuck to me for as long as I was in jail—and after I graduated from it as well.

Thirty-eight:

Saeed at the Court of a King

The day was coming to an end when a hand shaking my own woke me up. I found myself lying on a straw mattress in a dark, low-ceilinged room. The chamber was illuminated faintly by a little daylight forcing its way, wounded, through the netted and barred opening at the top of one wall.

The hand to my left was shaking mine and pressing it reassuringly. I found I was unable to move my fingers, so I turned my head to the left and saw a very long form lying there on a straw mattress like my own. He was naked, and at first sight his body seemed to have been painted with a deep red pigment.

Had it not been for his eyes smiling silently to me in encouragement, and for his hand pressing mine and telling me to be brave, I would have thought the body lying to my left was a corpse.

I said "Hello," but it came out "Ah!"

Then I heard the man clad in the crimson cloak of kingship whisper, "What's your story, brother?"

"Is this the cell?" I asked.

"Is this the first time?" he asked.

"There is a room without windows—"

"And there is a hope without walls—"

"What about you?" I asked him.

"I'm a *fedaiy,* a guerrilla and a refugee. And you?"

I did not know what to reveal about my identity before the

majestic figure laid out there who, when he spoke, did not groan and in fact spoke in order not to groan. Should I tell him I was a mere "sheep," one who had stayed on in the country, or should I confess that it was through crawling that I entered his court?

I disguised my shame by emitting a lengthy groan.

He forced himself to stand up. And I saw him bend his head down so that it would not hit the ceiling; or perhaps he was bending his tall figure down to look at me.

"Stop it, man!" he shouted suddenly.

Well, I told myself, I've become a man now that I've been thoroughly booted by jailers!

He seemed to be very young, his cloak of crimson only emphasizing his youth.

"Where do you hurt, brother?"

Had we met outside, would he have called me brother?

There was something about his eyes that took me back twenty years to the playground of my youth and the slopes of Jabal Street. In his voice, as he asked me where I hurt, I heard the screams of Yuaad when, so many ages ago, the soldiers hurled her into the car for deportation: "This is my country, this is my home, and this is my husband!"

I burst into tears, like a child.

"Patience, father."

I did not stop crying, but now it was from pride and gratitude; my tears were those of a soldier whose leader is awarding him a medal for courage.

"Be brave, father."

Trample all you like, you huge boots, on my chest! Suffocate me! And you, black room, crumble over my helpless body! Were it not for all of you, we would not have been reunited! Those brutish guards, if only they knew, were merely guards of honor at the court of this king. That dark and narrow room was the outer hall that led to this, the throne room!

I have become his brother! I have become his father! Laugh at that, if you can, my jailers!

A feeling of enormous pride spread over me, a pride I had never felt since the day that Yuaad had shouted, "This is my husband!"

I am your father, O King! I do have a son like you, but his cloak is of sea coral.

I did not want to tell him I was from Haifa and go into lengthy explanations, so I told him instead I was from Nazareth.

"We have every right to be proud of our brave people there," he said.

Then he asked, "A Communist, of course?"

"No, a friend of theirs."

"Fine, glad to meet you indeed."

He healed my wounds by talking about his own. He kept widening that single tiny window in the wall until it became a broad horizon that I had never seen before. Its netted bars became bridges to the moon, and between his bed and mine were hanging gardens. I told him of myself, what I had always aspired to for myself. I did not want to lie, but I did not want to soil the majesty of the moment by speaking of personal details: these the jailers had stripped from me when they stripped off my clothes. Here we were, one naked man facing another. Would Adam ever have left Paradise of his own free will?

The guards, however, did not leave me there. They removed me from Paradise and transferred me to a large hall in the prison where the inmates lay huddled together, each lying on a straw mattress on an iron bed. For many days I disobeyed the rules so that they would return me to the cell where I would meet again that young man who had called me father. But they did not.

I learned from the prisoners that he was a Palestinian *fedaiy* who had crossed over from Lebanon and had been taken prisoner when wounded.

They also told me that his name was Saeed. "Just like me," I commented.

"But he was never nicknamed Shakespeare!" they pointed out and smiled consolingly.

I occupied myself binding my wounds and looking out for this second Saeed until finally I met his sister, the second Yuaad, as I was leaving prison for the third time.

Thirty-nine:

Saeed Sings a Song of Bliss

Those who enter jail in our country become like a shuttle in a weaver's hand, ever coming in and going out. My weaver was the big man. My pure-white past did not so much atone for me as rather blacken my present all the more. I came, then, to see the jail's iron gate as a door connecting the two yards of one prison. In the inner yard, I would wander awhile, then rest; in the outer yard I would also wander awhile, then go back to jail.

While I was thus engaged in this process of shuttling to and fro, the big man came and threatened that they would keep on transferring me from one prison to another until I either died, whether in jail or not, or went back into their service.

"But why can't you get off my back and onto someone else's?" I demanded.

"Do you imagine we can find someone like you on every street corner?"

"I've spent half my life in your service. Let me live out the rest in quiet obscurity, like any one of God's children, peaceful and unimportant."

But he made me understand that there could be no release from their service until the day I died. He explained, "Your father gave it to you as his inheritance, and you will pass it on to your children.

They will curse you, but our long arm will reach them nevertheless, generation after generation."

He then warned me that people would not believe my repentance, saying that my inheritance would always get the best of me and that bad behavior learned young lasts until one dies. I had, he said, no one to turn to but him, and he threatened me with imprisonment, torture, and starvation.

But I did not starve. Instead I began selling vegetables from a stall in Wadi al-Nasnas, selling sweet red melons in season. When the municipal police were sent to pester me, I gave them some to eat. When the neighborhood kids threw stones at me because of my notorious reputation, I enjoyed it and they left me in peace.

All except the big man. He did not leave me in peace but had the authorities issue an order forbidding me to leave Haifa. I hid the order from the local police to keep their friendship. The big man, however, sent his own men to surprise me at my stall one noon. They led me off to prison after charging me publicly with having disobeyed the compulsory stay order. My going to Shafa Amr to buy melons, they said, had threatened the integrity of the state. Whoever, as they put it, transported red melons in secret could also carry radishes secretly and there was, after all, only a difference in color between red radishes and hand grenades! And red was not, under any circumstances, the same as blue and white. With a watermelon, moreover, one could blow up a whole regiment if grenades were hidden inside it. "Don't you see that, you mule?"

"But I cut the melons open with a knife so the buyer can see," the "mule" responded.

"Oh! Knives too, eh?" they exclaimed.

The news spread that a compulsory stay order had been issued me, and my stall became very popular. One day a young man carrying newspapers under his arm approached me and said, "Hello. So you got one, then?"

"I got one long ago," I answered.

"Then why don't you read our paper?"

"Because you didn't come earlier."

I did now display the compulsory order on the wall of my stall, but a couple of days later the police returned and told me that the governor had been kind enough to revoke the order, and that our state was a truly democratic one. They then tore it off the wall and returned me to prison on the grounds that I had shown disrespect for official state papers.

As one high official put it, "If you were in an Arab country, would you dare to show off a compulsory stay order? Our democracy is just not right for you people."

This comment was made as I was on my way to prison.

Later, emerging from the inner to the outer jail, after having been set free, that is, I stopped by the side of the road between Bisan and Affulah and tried to get a lift. A private car carrying a number plate with the Hebrew letter *sh* showing that it was registered in Shekkem, which is none other than Arab Nablus, came to a halt beside me. The driver invited me inside.

I sat in the back seat feeling very much alone. A girl was sitting up in front beside the driver. All I could see of her was her jet-black hair, as black as my own before it turned grey; and I pondered, at this thought. How one's mind can wander no matter what the situation.

Having traveled some distance, the driver astonished me by saying, "We went to visit a relative of ours in Shatta prison, but the warden denied his being there. Friends told us you have met Saeed. Do you know where he is?"

This question worried me. I felt for the door handle to get out of this explosive car, but it was speeding along too fast. I replied, stunned, not thinking, "I am Saeed!"

At this the girl with the jet-black hair turned and stared at me angrily, exclaiming, "No, my brother Saeed."

"Yuaad!"

"My darling!"

"Yuaad!"

At least that's the dialogue I now think took place between us. However, during those few, very brief moments, I neither heard nor saw anything but two green eyes shining with a heavenly light I had missed so much for twenty years.

Yes, I had seen Yuaad! Suddenly I had seen twenty years of Yuaad all at once. Her eyes, her voice, her hair, and her figure! How would a fish feel if a storm all at once broke away the ice that had been building for twenty years on the surface of its river? How do you think the soil beneath the South Pole would feel if the ice of all the ages were suddenly removed? Like volcanoes erupting in fire, and rocks exploding to release a stream—that's how I felt! I burst into tears.

They stopped the car. Yuaad got out and moved into the back seat next to me. She took my hands in hers and placed them on her breast, then laid her head on my shoulder and our tears mingled. The driver sang with the horn of his car and drove slowly, as if we were in a wedding procession.

"Saeed, Saeed!"

"Yuaad, Yuaad!"

"I have found him at last!"

"And you will never lose him again!"

"How is he?"

"As you see, Yuaad!"

A fierce desire gripped me to clap my hands, to sing, to ululate and scream until the layers of necessity, silence, humiliation, and submission were all gone. It had always been, "Yes, sir!"; "At your command, sir!" But now my spirit would fly free, and rise far into the sky where eagles soar, and cry out, "I am like you, people, brave like you; like you I can plant my feet firmly on the ground, my back straight, my figure tall, my head ascending to the sky. I am happy in my courage, like you, the people! And Yuaad is here at my side, young as a wild lily, fresh as an old dream!

For twenty long years I had lived alone, away from Yuaad. I had lived that time to its very last drop, to its very dregs. I had drunk its bitter cup and had left not a drop for her. I had saved her from those twenty bitter years so that she could remain young and twenty and not suffer the pain of those I had lived. She had returned to me as she had been, the same girl, crying and laughing, defying and loving and calling me "Saeed!"

I am happy, everyone! Listen to me, O world, from the Green Belt to the blue horizon, all of you deserts and fields, graves and skies. I am now free of both prisons, both the inner and the outer ones. Free at last!

137

"Saeed," my name indeed, "happy" at last!

But now I did something completely unexpected. I have no idea what came over me, but I suddenly opened the car door and threw myself out, my hand still clutching Yuaad's. We tumbled out onto the hard ground and I lost consciousness.

Forty:

Two Views on a Disaster Known as "The Cordon"

I awoke to the fresh, fragrant air of a village at evening. I found myself lying on a clean woolen mattress. My mind wandered back to my mother and how, as a child, I used to rest at her bosom in our old house. The aroma of foods stored in bulk, oil jugs, and an oven wafted toward me, and I heard whispers being suppressed, and the breathing of children sleeping peacefully.

Faintly I saw the shadowy figures of peasant women going and coming, carrying trays of saffron rice topped with chicken, and I could see a low wooden table in the middle of the ancient room.

"Mother!" I cried out.

I heard the women calling to Yuaad that her father had awakened. I began looking around for her father but could find no sign of him.

"Where am I?"

The women thanked God for my recovery as they retreated outside the room at Yuaad's request. I heard them asking her to be quick before the food got cold.

Yuaad knelt down on the mat near me and said, "Preserve my secret, out of your friendship for my brother Saeed!"

She told me we were in the village of Salakah[38], in the plain. This name is not on the map, not because it has ceased to exist, although this does happen, but because it never existed. The fact is I invented this name for the village that gave us shelter to preserve its curious secret which, although known to many, has been kept from the authorities for twenty years.

Yuaad's secret, a different one, was that she was pretending to our hosts that I was her father. "It has been said," I remarked, "that you've many a brother not born to your mother and I say that you've many a father not married to your mother."

"What a thing to say! May her soul rest in peace!"

"Well, what was it that kept you with me then? And where's the driver?"

She reported that when we fell from the car which was, thank God, moving very slowly, I had lost consciousness but had not been injured. Yuaad herself, whom I had been hugging tightly at the time, had landed on top of me and had not been hurt at all. Men and women from the village of Salakah working on a nearby kibbutz had hurried over; their leader, Abu Mahmoud, was our host. He had welcomed us and had brought us to his village and into his home. When they found that I was unconscious merely from exhaustion, they had left me to rest.

As for her friend, the car's owner-driver, Yuaad went on, he had been obliged to return to Nablus, for regulations forbade him from staying overnight in Israel with his car. He had very much regretted what might have appeared to be his negligence in leaving us, especially since he imagined that because he had not shut the car door properly he was therefore responsible for our fall. I kept my mouth tightly shut; I didn't want to take another fall now!

Yuaad had preferred to stay until I regained consciousness and told her more about where her brother Saeed might be. She had come all the way from Beirut to Shatta prison seeking him.

"And what about our resident 'prisoner of Zenda'?" by which I meant myself. "Won't you come back to him?"

"Now, father, it's dinnertime. Up you get, and honor with your presence those who are honoring us."

Members of the household were streaming in to greet the guests who had come, "from Arab countries." They welcomed us with great enthusiasm and hung on every word we uttered, as if each was a precious good smuggled from outside. It was Yuaad who answered their questions, while I contented myself with rising to greet people and returning their kindly comments, afraid my tongue might slip with some inappropriate remark.

Yuaad obviously could hold her own with any of the men present. She was young and beautiful, and, even more important, she knew just how to converse with men. I was fascinated watching her, and, hearing their compliments of her addressed to myself, I gave all praise and thanks to God while preserving our secret from them.

They told us they had done their best to hide our presence from the other villagers for fear that someone might inform on us, since they suspected that we were there illegally.

Our host, Abu Mahmoud, told us that the previous year the village had been put under a cordon for seven days while a search for infiltrators was carried out. When the authorities found none, they arrested fourteen men before lifting the cordon from the village.

But what was this cordon? Abu Mahmoud explained: "The police cordon off a village, blocking all exits and imposing a curfew. Then their armored cars race along the narrow lanes of the village, and they spread out, with bloodhounds, entering homes and terrorizing children, spilling oil jugs on sacks of flour in case the 'infiltrators' have slipped into the jugs or sacks.

"If we hear screaming coming from a house, we crawl there at dead of night. Nighttime in our village is dark indeed, and has been so for twenty years, kept so deliberately to conceal the authorities. But we too use the dark to cover our own activities. If the family of one of the homes afflicted reports that they have taken one of its members away we promptly help some other fugitive, using cover of night, to escape through the cordon to safety or to some means of earning a living."

"But is there no one to help the villagers?" Yuaad asked.

"No one except the Communists and the kibbutz people help us."

I had already noticed now villagers always think anyone they meet coming from "the Arab countries" is a Communist or a relative, and would welcome them most warmly as such. I laughed quietly to myself but merely commented, "You don't say! Praise be to God!"

Abu Mahmoud went on: "Now the Communists, their members of Parliament, do dare to penetrate the cordon. They come right through and give us their sympathy and encourage us to resist. And they collect facts and shout in the Knesset, which is rather like your parliament."

This last comment made me laugh to myself, all right.

"And," he continued, "they force the minister to answer them. That forces knowledge of our plight through the official wall of silence. They also lead demonstrations in Nazareth and Tel Aviv and shout, 'Remove the cordon! Remove the cordon!' And they publish reports of our cordon in their newspapers and tell us that the press of free peoples in all parts of the world quotes from them. They say that our cordon moves the conscience of the world, which Zionism would totally enclose in a cordon if it weren't for the Communists. Did you read about our cordon in the newspapers of the Arab countries, those which have not been cordoned off by Zionism?"

Yuaad, her eyes glittering in anger, commented, "The papers of the Arab world cordon us with news of 'victories,' like haloes over the heads of saints; there's no space for reports of your cordons. They've kept on encircling us with the cordons of their victories, until there's nothing but chaos and we can no longer differentiate between them and the wreaths of flowers set on graves."

"And Zionism raises hell all over the world for so much as a scratch on a finger!"

Yuaad, her anger thoroughly aroused, positively roared, "Gentlemen, that's enough from your viewpoint! You see utter calamity in what has happened to you, whereas our lives are now one big cordon. You have a phrase, 'from the cradle to the grave'; we have one that goes, 'from cordon to cordon!' Don't expect those living their entire lives within cordons, under constant inspection, at the mercy of every kind of bloodhound, deprived of their very roots, to have much sympathy with your particular 'calamity' when it has become the life experience of a whole nation, from the Gulf to the Atlantic!"

I could not restrain myself from remarking, "Your brother's match you surely are!"

Heads turned in my direction, apparently upset at my interruption. I was worried that I'd slipped up and so began distributing greetings left and right: "Praise God! Praise God, everyone!"

They muttered something like greetings in response.

"But what about the kibbutz people?" Yuaad now asked.

"After a week of cordon," Abu Mahmoud replied, "their lands yearn for our able hands. Then they intercede to have the cordon removed and we return to work in their fields."

"Why you in particular?" she asked.

"Because they were *our* fields, and it was we who planted them and we do so still. They love us and we love them. The authorities, you see, were unable to confiscate this friendship."

Suddenly my tongue slipped loose again and I found myself exclaiming in surprise: "Then all this greenery is the fruit of *your* labor, not at all as the big man claimed!"

Heads again turned my way, and people whispered to each other, "What big man?"

Yuaad hurriedly gave them her charming smile and explained that her father was simply talking about a big soldier, "with whom he had discussed politics on the way over the bridge to the West Bank."

She went on to reassure them that we had come across the bridge with official Israeli permission, and that we would remain a month in the country searching for her brother Saeed, whom we had heard was a prisoner in the notorious Shatta jail.

"The extremely notorious!" they added.

"Just you ask me about that," I remarked.

But a sudden din and confusion outside saved me from this last slip of my tongue.

Forty-one:

The Secret That Didn't Die When the Secret Did

Our hosts were now fussing about us so, welcoming us effusively as though we had just arrived, that the noise developing outside was drowned out. They were doing their best to disguise with smiles the gravity that now was apparent on their faces; it reminded me of soldiers using branches to camouflage their helmets or tanks. I was about to ask what had happened, but Yuaad trod hard on my foot. I held my tongue.

The women had begun to disappear. Little children who had been sleeping in a corner now woke up and, carrying their bedding, also disappeared. They kept their heads low as they walked, not looking up into the faces of their fathers gathered there.

Men we had not seen before began entering the reception room where we were and sat down after greeting us. But the men of the household began leaving, one by one, and did not come back. All except Abu Mahmoud, that is; he remained seated there quite motionless, his back so erect you could scarcely tell whether he was sitting or standing.

A heavy silence settled over us, like the calm that precedes a storm. I felt like saying, "Yet he's a tree no storm could uproot!" But Yuaad's foot kept pressing on mine, blocking my words.

Now we could hear a woman sobbing a little way off; but this seemed to make the men's expressions of welcome for us all the louder. They kept up a veritable endless chorus of greetings. Again and again they stood to welcome us, with me continually rising in response, though still unable to withdraw my foot from beneath Yuaad's or to release my now-imprisoned tongue.

Finally our host left, doing his best to walk away naturally but managing only a military-looking march. Soon, however, he was back and spoke the koranic phrase invoked at times of death or disaster, "to God alone is all power, all permanence."

"Everything okay?" I couldn't resist asking, anxiously.

"A venerable old gentleman, a member of our family, died this evening, and the women are weeping for him."

Having now discovered that it was all right for me to speak, I next asked, "The village headman, was he?"

One of the newcomers merely responded, "God the most merciful has taken him unto Himself."

"I wish to God he'd take all the authorities!" I dared to comment.

"We must all return to dust," the same old man responded.

"God have mercy on him! And his children do live on after him," Yuaad consoled all present.

I had feared, when I saw people looking worried after all the noise and confusion outside, that someone had come to tell these people the truth about me. Hearing all this about a man having died, I was therefore most relieved and couldn't prevent yet another idiomatic expression escaping from my lips, namely, "Thanks be to God. He's saved the day!"

This time Yuaad didn't anticipate my blunder, and her foot pressed mine too late to prevent this last utterance. But, amazingly, those present muttered their approval of what I had said. So now I quite defied Yuaad's foot and went on to explain the philosophy of our family, the Pessoptimists, how there is a kind of death which is better than another, and one, indeed, better than life itself. I related how my elder brother had been killed by a crane and pieces of his body had been lost in the port of Haifa, so that we finally buried his body without his head.

Again the gathering seemed to approve of my ancient family

philosophy. I busied my mind preparing pertinent questions concerning the ancestry of those present, for, who could say, our family trees might well be intertwined at some point or other since we all did, after all, descend from Adam.

But Yuaad stopped me from indulging in these mental-historical gymnastics by giving me a light hug and whispering, "Uncle Saeed, Uncle Saeed, it was you I came to visit!"

"You mean only to visit?" I burst aloud.

Abu Mahmoud, our host, misinterpreting, interrupted, "No, you don't have to pay your respects to him; we've already buried him and the wake is now over." He must have thought we were discussing visiting his dead relative, not Yuaad's visiting the living—namely, myself.

"You mean the burial took place this evening?" I asked.

"Yes, this evening."

"But why didn't you wait until dawn?"

"Oh, there will be no dawn for him tomorrow."

What dawn was he speaking about, I wondered. Quite perplexed, I commented: "I don't understand a word you're saying."

"The authorities don't understand either!" he replied.

"But we're your friends," Yuaad insisted. "Please explain. Silence means suffocation for you."

"Well," Abu Mahmoud began, "everything around us villagers is silent—the earth, the animals, and the plow. Our language is that of silence. We inherit it generation after generation. If you learn to speak that language, then we'll understand one another."

"But don't you ever celebrate, really let yourselves go in song and rejoicing?" Yuaad asked.

"The problem, I'm afraid, is more complex than you, a lady from Beirut, could imagine. We have sung and sung and sung, like none ever did before. But our wedding celebrations always end up like funerals. Those we think are our friends always abduct the bride and flee to Beirut."

"But nowadays your friends are different. They are loyal and sincere. Didn't you yourself earlier make favorable mention of the Communists?"

"Yes, we do regard them highly. But olive oil is our basic food.

146

We do enjoy thorn sticks but they have a tendency to break. Lightning isn't bad, either, but it can't relieve the gloom of our silent nights. We shall keep on and on testing them in silence until they do give us of their olives to eat. Don't forget that it's not the crowing of cocks that brings each dawn. But our cocks will crow all right when they do bring it about. It is up to our friends, therefore, to learn to speak our language, that of the earth, of the animals, and of the plow—a determined silence."

Throughout this explanation the other visitors there nodded their heads in quiet approval. I felt like interrupting him with the objection "If what you say is true, then I, Saeed Pessoptimist, ever silent in humiliation, must be the peasants' first and foremost friend." But then I remembered how my past deeds would speak only too loudly for me, how I had always informed on people and had never held my silence. At this point a curious idea struck me; it was that I, for all my great expertise as an informer, was never able to inform on any man who had kept his silence. So I shut up!

While I was engaged in this silent conversation with myself, a woman, thin and dry, like a stalk of dead maize, burst in, tears streaming, and cried out, "The Secret's dead! Abu Mahmoud, why cover up any longer?"

Abu Mahmoud rushed over to her, gripped her tightly, and tried to force her outside. But she resisted him strongly. So he remained there holding her and, resting his head on her breast, suddenly burst into tears himself, just like a child. Trying to console him, she wept with him, while we all felt absolutely stunned. Now the visitors began leaving, one by one, and went outside where they were swallowed by the thick black night. They seemed to be saying: "The Secret may be dead, but we have to live tomorrow!"

That whole night we spent listening to Abu Mahmoud's amazing tale. It was about a young blind man from the village who had left in 1948 with those streams of refugees who had flowed out into all the vastness of the Arab world. Later, after the establishment of the state, he had infiltrated back home. The villagers had kept the fact of his return a secret. They had given him shelter and food, and he had earned his living making mats and brooms. They had even arranged his marriage, to a woman they pretended was his brother's second wife; her children, they claimed, belonged to his brother. They had all kept the secret for years,—they, their children and grandchildren. Information about this secret still failed to reach the authorities despite all the cordons imposed throughout the past twenty years. When one village chief died and another was appointed in his place, he would tell them as much as they wanted to know about any of the others, but nothing of him. It developed into an established tradition, one never to be misused by any member of the village. It was, in fact, much like the awakening of a conscience to something never before aroused.

But at last the Secret had died, that night in fact. So they had buried him silently and now mourned him quietly.

"Who was that woman who burst into the room?"

"His widow."

"And who is she to you, Abu Mahmoud?"

"My mother."

"Please, don't take it so hard. He lived a full life. May his soul rest in peace."

"But I have not. Everyone used to say he was my father, but I would deny this to live."

"No, so that he might live."

"Well, this is my secret, which is not dead yet, though he is."

Dawn had now arrived.

Forty-two:

Yuaad's Return to the Old House

It was while we sat in a restaurant in Affulah, about to begin a breakfast of chickpeas and beans, that I started to have my doubts about Yuaad. She was surprised to discover that Jews from Europe were so well able to prepare our traditional Arab food we had ordered. The fact was, however, as I pointed out, that they had come chiefly from the Arab world. Nothing had really changed for them, not even their use of swear words; they also swore and cursed superbly in Arabic.

Yuaad laughed when I pointed this out and swore at me affectionately.

"What! A daughter swear at her father?" I joked.

"But you're my uncle, and the knight of my dreams ever since I was a child," she responded.

"I'm sure that He who changed me overnight from your father to your uncle will bring back your memory this evening. Come along with me to Haifa; let's take up where we left off."

In the car driving us to Haifa, Yuaad began speaking to me in a particularly kind and understanding tone and announced, "I'm going to tell you something you'll find really amazing; and you'll be the one to judge whether the surprise is good or bad."

With a manner like that of a teacher addressing a student, she

149

began a tale I simply could not believe. On and on she went, with me breaking in from time to time with comments of, "Impossible!"

She said I had been mistaken about her, that I had confused her with the Yuaad I had been waiting for, a woman who was in fact her mother! And she was now dead.

"Yes, Uncle, I am the daughter of that Yuaad you were waiting for!"

"Impossible! Impossible!"

"Do I resemble her so very much, uncle?"

"Impossible! Impossible!"

She told me that her mother had always spoken well of me. She had named her son Saeed after me, and her daughter Yuaad after herself. This was so her daughter, if one day she returned to the land of her own birth, could tell me that life in another country had not changed them.

"And now," Yuaad continued, "we have met, uncle. And did we change?"

"Youth is youth and never changes. But I do see, much to my regret, that time, for all its being defeated by your youth, has taken its revenge on your memory. How else could a lover forget her first love, the flower fail to remember the dawn that gave form to its bud."

"Did you really love her that much, uncle?"

"I love you as much as an old man would love his past to be only a dream from which he is awaking. I am now awake; how is it I find you still hallucinating in your sleep?"

I plunged deep into fantasy, like a drowning man diving into an underwater cave where he thinks he sees some distant light. She would, I thought wake up when she entered my old house in Haifa.

When we arrived there, I took her by the arm and led her up the stairs, those same steps down which they had hurled her some twenty years before. I felt like a bridegroom on his wedding night. I simply tossed those twenty lost years in the garbage can in the courtyard and flew up those stairs as if on wings, inspired by the presence of Yuaad. "Here we are again," I kept exclaiming, "returning victorious!"

The neighbors were opening their doors to greet us and to ask us what was the matter. And Yuaad, running at my side, responded to their greetings by explaining proudly, "It's my uncle. I've not seen him for ages!"

One of our neighbors began to ululate for joy and others joined in, the sounds of their celebration coming in succession, like the signaling of ships' horns in the port of Haifa at midnight on New Year's Eve.

When we entered the house, Yuaad, out of breath, said: "You can rest now. You're the victor and I'm your prisoner!" Then she asked, "What were the women celebrating?"

"Your return."

"As a prisoner?"

"As a visitor."

"But why are they so pleased?"

"Prisoners always shave and wash and celebrate on visiting days."

"But this is not time for celebration."

"You would deny these prisoners the joy of a visit?"

"How can happiness ever come in the presence of a conqueror?"

"Just as food cooks in the presence of a fire."

She asked me what was the source of all my wisdom, and I told her it had come from prison guards who had given me lessons in Shakespeare. I related my prison experiences with the guards, and how I had met her brother in my cell. I told her how he had spoken words that made me see it as a paradise, the bars on its window as a bridge to the moon.

Sometimes she laughed: at others cried. Finally she said, "Tell me about your Yuaad."

And I did tell her our story how, "We sat together right here. And over here, in this room, you stayed awake waiting for me while I remained in the other room, like a fool holding my breath, until the soldiers finally came."

"The soldiers! They've put a cordon round the house!"

This shout came from a neighbor who had forced her way in through the door without permission. She found me kneeling on all fours at Yuaad's feet, reenacting that first fall of mine on the stairs twenty years before, and Yuaad sitting before me, watching and laughing.

I did not rise from where I knelt.

Forty-three:

Awaiting a Third Yuaad

Yuaad remained in her chair, legs crossed like a man, and said, "Get up and give me a cigarette. Don't be afraid."

"But they'll take you away again, like they did before."

"It was my mother they took away then."

"But it's you they'll take this time."

"No, things are different now."

"But they haven't changed."

"If they haven't, that's their tragedy. But we have."

"You won't be able to fend them off. They'll take you from me!"

"Where?"

"To some country not your own."

"But I'm going back to a country that isn't my own anyway. Do you have another solution?"

"You could hide at a neighbour's."

"For how long?"

"We'll do the same as that blind man in the village of Salakah."

"For twenty years, you mean?"

"Until things change."

"But who will change them?"

"Your brother, Saeed, said that the people would."

"The people will take action while the people hide away?"

"You and I will hide, but your brother Saeed will be in active combat."

"And then he'll donate freedom, as a gift, to those who hide?" Yuaad laughed sarcastically, then went on. "If you remain alive, Uncle Saeed, you'll be seventy by the time you meet the third Yuaad. But you won't recognize her, nor will she recognize you."

She sat me down at her side and asked, "Do you love me, uncle?"

"With all the anguish of my life."

"Would you like to marry me?"

"Until death us do part."

"Should I marry an old man, coming to the end of his life?"

"But I'll return to the beginning."

"Impossible!"

"Then how can your brother believe that things will return to where they began?"

"He got that idea from his elders; of his beginning an old man remembers only the prime of youth and so thinks fondly of it. Do you really know how the beginning was, uncle? The beginning was not merely sweet memories of pines over Mount Carmel, or orange groves, or the songs of Jaffa's sailors. And did they really sing anyway?

"Do you really want to return to the beginning, to mourn your brother torn to pieces by the crane as he carved his living from the rocks. You want to do it all again, from the beginning?"

"But your brother, Saeed, said they had learned from the mistakes of their predecessors and would not commit them again."

"If they had really learned, they wouldn't have spoken at all of returning to the beginning."

"You're so young for so much wisdom, Yuaad; wherever did you acquire it?"

"From my long life that is still before me."

"Will you be leaving me?"

"Water cannot truly ever leave the sea, uncle. It evaporates, then returns in winter in the springs and rivers. It will always return."

"Will I remain alone then?"

"Even the blind man of Salakah did not live alone. Go and make mats in his village."

But I did not go to the village of Salakah and make mats, neither there nor anywhere else. For the soldiers came. I just remained there, without moving. Except that I did put my hands over my eyes, covering them so I would not see the end as I had seen the beginning.

I felt the hands of soldiers push me outside and hurl me onto the stairs. Then I found myself stretched out at the foot of the stairway. But this time I didn't shout for help from my friend Jacob. He was the one who needed help now.

From above, from my house, I heard a woman screaming and the noise of kicks and punches, a frightful din. A violent battle raged between Yuaad and the soldiers, and I saw her resist, shouting and kicking and biting the shoulder of one soldier who cried out and retreated. Then I saw them all charge together and force her into the deportation van. As the door was closed, I heard her shout, "Saeed, don't worry! I will return!"

Then I opened my eyes, sighed deeply, and said, "So here we are, back again at the beginning."

But I witnessed a strange situation develop. I saw a police officer go over Yuaad's papers respectfully, and heard him apologize for the orders he had canceling her permit to enter Israel and requiring her to return at once with them to Nablus. He added that next day she would have to go back from where she had come, across the bridge to Jordan.

I heard her comment, "I expected nothing different from you."

"Well, we didn't expect you to stay at Saeed's."

"This is my country, this is my home, and this is my uncle!" she retorted.

"This," I told myself, "I shall treasure as food for the next twenty years!"

"But that's prohibited," I heard him say. She went on to ask why, since she expected no other treatment from them, they expected anything different from her.

The officer bowed with military politeness and said, "My pretty young lady, we expect from you even more than you do."

Yuaad shook hands with me and bade me farewell. Then she brought her face close to mine and asked, "Did you kiss my mother before she left?"

"No. They were standing between us."

"In that case you have missed the second kiss, too."

Then she was gone.

Forty-four:

The Glorious Finale—Gripping the Stake

As I just said, dear sir, I did not go to that village of Salakah and make mats, neither there nor anywhere else. What I did was return to the stake.

Yes, there I was again, sitting cross-legged and alone on top of that blunt stake. Night after night bad dreams pursued me, but I had strength neither to fend them off nor to wake up. Yes, the same old nightmare about a stake, and the same old obsessive fear—what if it turned out not to be a nightmare at all. I put on another heavy blanket but the chill pierced it too. Another and another I added until I had seven over me, but all were pierced by the cold. "Where is the beautiful princess who will do away with all these covers and warm me?" I often cried.

But the soldiers had once more taken her away. Again and again I murmured her name, blaming her bitterly for my fate, for it was she who had convinced me that my past stake was not a nightmare. How, then, was I to believe that my present stake *was* one. Yes, a Yuaad had returned, but not my Yuaad. She was a bouquet of roses for a wedding of the future, and yet also a wreath of fresh flowers on the grave of the past. For twenty years I had awaited her return, but when she did come she said, "I am not your Yuaad." Then she left me alone, while insisting that I was not really alone. To my question of whether she would return she had replied, "Yes, as the waters of the sea return to it, in winter."

Winter arrived. "Yuaad, please come back!" I pleaded.

"This is your winter alone," was her reply.

So, alone again and high up on that stake, I gazed down at all God's creation.

And one by one they came to me.

Jacob, my old friend, came first. He was sad. I shouted down to him, "The stake, old friend of a lifetime, do something!"

"But we all sit on one!" was his reply.

"I don't see you on one," I objected.

"And we see no one else's either. Each of us is alone, on his own stake. That is the stake we share," he explained, then left.

The big man came too, looking very perplexed. I shouted to him, "The stake, sir!"

"That's not a stake," he replied. "It's a television antenna. Each and every one of you acts as if he were in a submarine; the deeper you go, the higher its periscope rises. Just sit there and relax, why don't you!" Then he left.

The young man who always has a newspaper tucked under his arm also appeared. I shouted to him, "The stake, my son!"

"Those who don't want to sit on it must come down into the streets, with us. There is no third choice."

And with that, off he went along the street.

Is there, then, no place under the sun for me but this stake? Isn't there at least a lower stake where I can sit? A quarter stake, half a stake, a three-quarter stake?

The first Yuaad passed by. I stretched out my hand to her to pull her up, but she gripped me fast and began dragging me down to an exile's grave. But I held on tight to my stake.

And Baqiyya arrived, calling to me to descend. Walaa, she said, had built me a palace of sea shells there at his side. But I still gripped my stake.

Saeed, the son of Yuaad and brother of Yuaad, also came, waving his crimson cloak and calling, "Come on over, father; I shall warm you with my cloak." But I held on tight to my stake.

Then I saw the young man with the newspaper again, now with

an axe under his arm. I watched him swing his axe at the base of the stake as he cried, "I want to save you!" But I shouted down at him to stop, otherwise I would fall. And I held on to my stake all the tighter.

There I sat, my back hunched over, utterly perplexed as to what to do, when suddenly the figure of a man appeared. He was so tall that he reached right up to me, high though I was. He approached me very slowly, like a stray cloud. Of his face I saw only wrinkles, as on the surface of the sea when it is rippled by a wind from the east. But I recognized him instantly, and my heart burst with joy. Had I not feared falling, I would have hurled myself onto him, kissing his cheek.

"My master!" I shouted, "chief of all those of outer space, I have no one but you!"

"I know that," he replied.

"You came just in time."

"I only come to you just in the nick of time."

"Save me, reverend," I pleaded.

"I just wanted to say to you: this is the way you always are. When you can bear the misery of your reality no longer but will not pay the price necessary to change it, only then you come to me.

"But I can see that this problem has now become yours alone. So speak the words, 'If God wills it,' then climb on my back and let's go."

We flew off together, he bearing me on his back and I immersed in quiet communion with my ancestral spirits, from my first forebear, Abjar the son of Abjar, right on down to my uncle who had found the family treasure. I called upon them all to rally to me, to witness in pride their conquering son.

Then suddenly, down on earth beneath me, I heard the sound of joyful ululation. I gazed down and saw the young man, newspaper under his arm, still carrying his axe. There too were Yuaad and her brother, Saeed, along with Abu Mahmoud, the villager, his children carrying their bedding as they got up. The women who had been our neighbors were all celebrating loudly. There too was Acht, the worker in the Jimal valley, still carrying his lunch pail off to work, and Jacob, who had now descended from his own stake. And there was old Umm Asaad, the one who had been "had" in the census; even she was ululating now.

Finally, there was Yuaad. As she raised her head to the sky and pointed to us, I heard her say, "When this cloud passes, the sun will shine once more!"

EPILOGUE:
FOR THE SAKE OF TRUTH
AND HISTORY

The gentleman who received these strange letters wishes to inform you that when they reached him they bore the postmark of Acre. And so it was there that he pursued their author. Finally the trail led him to the mental hospital within the city walls, on the seashore.

The hospital staff welcomed him warmly. They took the opportunity to ask him to report their exasperation with the government for insisting on keeping the hospital in that same building which, during the British mandate, had been a notorious prison. There the British government had kept an execution chamber where they had hanged a number of the fighters in the Etzel, the paramilitary nationalist organization. That chamber, following the establishment of the state, had become a museum dedicated to the preservation of their memory. The staff thought the dignity of this shrine was being slighted by the presence of a mental hospital in the same building.

The gentleman who received these strange writings claims to have expressed astonishment, right there before the hospital staff, that there was no mention in that museum chamber of the Arabs whom the British had hanged there as well.

"But that," they responded, "is the responsibility of their own people."

"What do you mean?"

"Let them learn to take care of their cemeteries first."

"But are they allowed to visit those?"

"That's another matter altogether."

At this point the gentleman who received these strange missives moved on to another subject, to the problem he had come to solve by visiting the mental hospital. This, of course, was to discover who Saeed Pessoptimist, the Ill-fated, might really be.

They searched the hospital records of all those who had been inmates since the establishment of the state but could find no such name. They looked for the name closest to his and did find one that looked suspicious. This was a Saadi al-Nahhas, known as Abu al-Thum, referred to by some as Abu al-Shum. They did remember, moreover, that a young woman had visited the hospital recently and had asked about him, saying that she was a relative of his and had come from Beirut, across the bridge. But they had told her that he had died about a year before. To this she responded, "Well, so he's resting now and has left everyone else in peace!"

Then she had gone home, they said, over the bridge.

And so the gentleman who received these strange letters left that place.

It is now his hope that you will help him search for Saeed.

But where should one look?

If you should believe that tale about his taking refuge with his "brothers" from outer space, and were to look for him in the ancient catacombs of Acre, you might be like the lawyer who listened to a madman and went searching for buried treasure under a molasses tree. He kept on digging and digging, so the story goes, to the east, to the north, to the south, and to the west, until finally he completely uprooted the tree. But still he found no treasure.

The madman, in the meantime, was busy painting a wall with a brush dipped into a bucket with no bottom. When the lawyer returned, sweat streaming, the madman asked, "Well, did you uproot the tree?"

"Yes, I did," the lawyer replied. "I uprooted it completely, but I didn't find your treasure."

"Get yourself a brush and a bottomless bucket and stand next to me and do some painting," the madman suggested.

The point is, gentlemen, how will you ever find him unless you happen to trip right over him?

TRANSLATORS' NOTES

1. Two ancient Arabian tribes described in the Koran as having been destroyed by God. Their names are often met in classical Arabic literature as reminders of the impermanence of human power.

2. A Mamluk sultan (d. 1260) of Egypt who won great victories over the Mongols. His defeat of them at Ain Jalut in 1260 established his control over all Syria. That same year, however, Qutuz was assassinated by Baybars, the commander of his armies.

3. The hero of an ancient epic folk tale which relates the adventures of the Banū Hilāl tribe in Arabia and North Africa. Although still popular in the folk culture, Arab intellectuals, such as the poet Nizār Qabbānī and Habībī here, have recently come to ridicule the mythical heroism Abū Zaid represents, and to demand a more factual heroism from their leaders.

4. A Mamluk army commander and later sultan of Egypt during the period of the Crusades. His defeats of the Crusaders and successes over those conspiring against him internally were to be romanticized in a famous Arabic epic tale. Here the reference refers to his murder of his sultan Qutuz (see note 2 above). Baybars, disappointed in his expectation that Qutuz would reward him for the victory at Ain Jalut by granting him governorship over Aleppo, conspired against his sovereign's life. At an audience with the sultan he requested and was granted a captured Mongol girl. Baybars' bow to kiss the sultan's hand in thanks was a prearranged signal to his fellow conspirators who promptly attacked and killed Qutuz.

5. A descendant (1336–1404) of the Mongol leader Genghis

164

Khan and the conqueror of Asia. His invasions of enemy territory were marked, historians report, by great brutality and he is said to have built large pyramidal heaps of the skulls of his soldiers' victims.

6. In Hebrew this name means "broker."

7. This name, an invention of the author, means "will return" and, in colloquial Arabic, "again," "once more." There is play on both meanings in this book.

8. Salāh al-Dīn or Saladin (1138–1193), the army commander of Kurdish origins who became ruler of Egypt and Syria, is revered in Arab history as the liberator of much Arab territory from Crusader occupation. His relationship with his enemy Richard I (the Lionhearted) has been the subject of many Arabic legends.

9. An Andalusian geographer (1145–1217), man of letters and poet; he travelled several times to the Orient and his important *Travels of Ibn Jubair* (c. 1185) is a record of one of these trips.

10. Of the villages mentioned in the following scene El Manshiyeh (al-Manshiyya), Erwiass (Ruwais), Ikrit (Iqrit), Ad-Damun (al-Damun), Me'ar (Miy'ār) and El Gabseyeh (al-Ghābisiyya) have been destroyed, Kweikat (Kwaykāt), El Kabri, Sa'sa' (Saasaa), Ber'em (Kufr Bir'im) and Faradeh (Farradi) became kibbutzim, Elbirweh (Berwah), Deir El Kasy (Dair el-Qasi), Sahmata (Suhmata), Ez-Zeeb (al-Zeeb), Safsaf (al-Safsaf), Elbassa (al-Bassa), and Kofor E'enen (Kufr'Inān) became moshavs, *i.e.*, privately owned Jewish villages, and only El Mazra'ah (Mazraa) and Sha'ab (Shaab) remain Arab. For details of the fate of these and of the other villages mentioned in the text see *The Shahak Report* by Israel Shahak, Washington, n.d., first published in 1973 by Israel, and Anīs Sāyigh *Buldāniyyat Falastīn al-Muhtallah* (1948–67) (Existing Towns and Villages of Occupied Palestine), Beirut, 1968, and the *Atlas of Israel*, Ministry of Labor, Jerusalem, 1970. The spellings of the villages above are as given in Shahak, while those presented in parentheses are those adopted for this text.

11. The Mamluk sultan (1223–1290) of Egypt and Syria who, having repelled Mongol attacks on Syria turned on the Crusaders and captured in 1289 the well-fortified port city of Tripoli. He died while preparing to attack Acre, and it was his successor, his son al-Malik al-Ashraf, who captured the remaining cities under occupa-

tion. His defeat of the European garrison at Jerusalem (May 1291) brought a final end to Crusader rule in Syria and Palestine.

12. Elected Great Khan in 1251, Mangu Khan (1208–1259) became heir to a vast Mongol empire. He died of disease while advancing against China.

13. Brother of Mangu Khan and grandson of Genghis Khan, Hulagu (1217–1265) was sent to invade Persia and the Arab lands. Having rapidly defeated the rebellious Isma'ilis in Persia and besieged and sacked Baghdad (1258), he advanced on Syria where he conquered Aleppo and received the surrender of Damascus. On the death of his brother Mangu Khan he returned to Mongolia and the armies he left behind in Syria were routed at Ain Jalut by those of the Egyptian sultan Qutuz, under their commander Baybars.

14. The reference is to a rumor that circulated in the Arab world after the death of King Faisal I that he had been poisoned.

15. Muhyī al-Dīn ibn al-'Arabī (1165–1240) was one of the greatest Sufis (mystics) of Islam. He believed that God is an existence free of all attributes, and preached the idea of the unity of the universe. Andalusian by birth, he spent the last years of his life in Damascus, where he is buried. He left numerous works.

16. An Andalusian scholar, poet and inventor (d. 887 A.D.) Ibn Firnās is credited with developing the manufacture of crystal and with having experimented with flight by wearing a feather suit and wings and gliding from a precipice.

17. Known in Arabic as Ibn Rushd, Averroes (1058–1126) was an Andalusian scholar, a scientist proficient in physics, medicine, biology and astronomy as well as a theologian and philosopher.

18. Known in the West as Albategni, al-Bitānī al-Harrānī (d. 929) was a prominent astronomer. He made many discoveries pertaining to the lunar and solar systems.

19. One of the greatest scholars and most original minds of medieval Islam, al-Bīrūnī (d. 1078) made contributions to mathematics, astronomy, geography, history and linguistics.

20. A prolific engineer from Basra, al-Haytham (996–1039) wrote works on mathematics, physics, medicine and philosophy.

21. In Arabic the word means a 'doe.'

22. The most famous of pre-Islamic poets, he was the son of

a Yemeni prince. The verses refer to the poet's visit to Justinian I in Constantinople in quest of aid from the Byzantine monarch against the Persians. 'Caesar' here refers to Justinian.

23. Lt. Gen. Sir John Bagot Glubb, b. 1897. After graduation from the British Royal Military College and action in World War I in France, he served the newly established monarchy in Iraq from 1920 to 1930. Transferred to Trans-Jordan in 1930, he was appointed Chief of General Staff of the Arab Legion there from 1939 to 1956, when Arab nationalist agitation against him led to his dismissal by King Hussain of Jordan. The reference here reiterates a widely held Arab view that Glubb, when commander of the only fully armed and trained Arab army in the fighting of 1948, actually facilitated Zionist occupation of Palestine. Glubb has maintained, in his *A Soldier with the Arabs* (London, 1957) and elsewhere, that Israel failed at that time to extend its control further, and particularly over the West Bank, only because of the effectiveness of the Arab Legion troops he commanded.

24. Presumably a reference to the great losses suffered by the forces of Napoleon Bonaparte during his abortive attempt to conquer Acre in March, 1799.

25. This is a reference to the "Suez War" of 1956, when Britain and France, feeling threatened by President Nasser's nationalization of the Suez Canal, agreed that Israel should overrun Sinai, giving them the pretext of occupying the canal to "separate the warring parties."

26. Schneller was a German-run school in Jerusalem; Habibi's sarcasm and Saeed's idiocy are evident.

27. In Arabic the word means "sergeant."

28. The name in Arabic means "the one who remains."

29. On Ibn Jubair, see footnote 9 above.

30. Al-Mutanabbī (915–965) was one of the greatest and most popular Arab poets.

31. The Ismāʿīlīs developed from the Shīʿa sect of Islam as early as the middle of the eighth century. They considered that only an elite could be properly instructed in complex philosophical and theological theories and from this developed the belief, here also dem-

onstrated, that the Ismāʿīlī community allowed its adherents differing levels of initiation into its belief system.

32. A secret society in Baghdad of the eleventh century A.D., they believed that religion gains from "purification" by philosophical interpretation. They sought a synthesis between Greek philosophy and the principles and jurisprudence of Islam. Their doctrine sought to secure man's happiness, primarily in the next world, through a process of regaining the soul's "original purity" and then allowing it to be guided in its ascent by the Imām, *i.e.*, the leader of the sect.

33. He led a rebellion against the rule of the Fatimid Caliph of Egypt who had adopted the title Ruler in the Name of God. Abū Rakwah gave himelf the title Rebel in the Name of God; revered by his supporters for his courage and spirituality he was ultimately captured and executed by the Fatimid Caliph.

34. Following eviction of its Arab population Tantura was transformed into a *moshav* and is now named Dov.

35. Of the following villages El Mazar (al-Muzar), Breka (al-Buraikah), Um Khaled (Umm Khalid), Khribit Ez-Zababdeh (Khirbat al-Zababidah) and Jaleel Esh-Shamalieh (Jalil al-Shamaliyyah) have been destroyed, Et-Tireh (al-Tirah), Jabaʿa (Jabaʿ), Igzim (Ijzim), Kofor Lam (Kufr Lam), Ain Gazal (ʿAin Ghazal), and El Burje (Khirbat al-Burj) have become 'moghaus', Ein Houd (ʿAin Hawd), Kisaryah (Qaisariyyah), and El-Haram (al-Haram) have become Jewish suburbs and resort towns while Sarafend (now Tsirfin) has become a military camp. See also note 10 above.

36. ʿAlī ibn Abī Tālib (600–661) was a cousin and son-in-law of the Prophet and ruled as fourth Orthodox Caliph from 656–661. The seizure of part of the Caliphate by the Umayyad Muʾāwiyya in 659, followed by the assassination of ʿAlī in Kufa, the suspicious death of his son al-Hasan in 670, and the murder of his second son al-Husain at Karbala in 682, caused a rift among Muslims into a Sunni (orthodox) majority and a Shiʿa (followers of ʿAlī) minority that continues to this day. As this text shows, invocation of ʾAlī's name conjures up an image of integrity and compassion.

37. A Palestinian lawyer and orator, he was the first choice of the League of Arab States to organize and head the Palestine Liberation

Organization, which was officially formed in 1965. He was ultimately replaced in the leadership by Yasser Arafat.

38. The author may perhaps have chosen this name in reference to al-Sulaik ibn al-Sulkah (d. 605), a pre-Islamic vagabond poet famous for the quickness of foot and thorough knowledge of the Arabian terrain that enabled him to evade capture by the authorities. Such "vagabond poets" have a "Robin Hood" aura, and are popularly credited with providing help for the needy.

Interlink International Fiction

The best way to learn about people and places far away

This series is designed to bring to North American readers the once-unheard voices of writers who have achieved wide acclaim at home, but have not been recognized beyond the borders of their native lands. It publishes the best of the world's contemporary literature in translation and in original English.

Already published in the series

For a complete catalog please write to:
INTERLINK PUBLISHING
46 Crosby Street, Northampton, MA 01060
Tel: (413) 582-7054 Fax: (413) 582-7057 e-mail: info@interlinkbooks.com
website: www.interlinkbooks.com